ZACHARY BALL

KEP

HOLIDAY HOUSE, NEW YORK

Affectionately Dedicated to
Our June

CONTENTS

chapter one

DUCK HUNT

"I bet it won't be daylight for near-'bout another hour," the boy said.

His shotgun was over his left shoulder and he carried a battered old flashlight in his right hand. Every few seconds he would thumb the light, sending its weak beam down the swamp path ahead of his father, who was walking in front. The boy had been turning it on and off as they needed it since leaving the house, doing it that way to conserve the battery.

Bert Lanning, the father, carried a pair of boat oars over his shoulder and his shotgun in the crook of his left arm. He spoke to his son through the darkness.

"Yuh reckon that pup will sure-'nough retrieve, Kep?"

"Mr. Smath said he would." Kep's flashlight beam picked up the black spaniel scurrying through the path-side weeds. "I won't buy him unless he can. I ain't paid anything on him yet. I ain't even said for sure I'd take him." He flashed the beam down the path. "I'd sure-'nough like to buy him, though."

Bert Lanning was touched by the yearning in his son's tone. The boy ought to have him a dog, he was thinking, and wished he could buy this one for him. Kep was a good kid. He'd never had much he could call his own. And this past year, since Grace had died, it seemed like there'd been barely enough food to keep them alive.

"I'd not have too much trouble scaring me up fifteen bucks," Kep said, "if he turns out to be a good retriever. Especially if I get that Saturday job at the sawmill. You be sure and ask Mr. Norton about giving me that work, Pa, will you?"

"Yeah, I'll ask him."

"And that dollar a week I get from Mrs. Ames for running errands and stuff for her. That'll help," Kep went on. "Mr. Smath said I could pay just a little along as I got it." He flashed his light down the path. "Where is Bud, anyway? Is he on ahead?"

"Out in the brush somewheres. Yuh know, runnin' off thataway, snortin' around in the weeds, I'm wonder-in' if he'll retrieve or not."

10

"Well, we'll soon see," Kep said.

His excitement was a live thing within him now, and he didn't want to speculate about the spaniel any more. Not for a while anyway. Always if he tried to think something out when he was real excited, he never could do it. It was like trying to sketch out something with a pencil when it wasn't clear in your mind.

"Flash your light once," his pa said. "I can't see my hand in front of me."

Kep turned the light beam on the path ahead for a moment.

"You're pretty sure there'll be ducks this morning, Pa?" he asked.

"There'll be ducks," his father assured him. "This is duck weather."

Kep flashed his light down the path again. "Hey, look, Pa! Bud knows we're going in the boat! He's waiting there for us!"

They came to their old rowboat and the spaniel leaped in without waiting to be told.

Kep laughed. "He wants to go, all right. Don't you, boy?" He scuffed the dog's silky ears as he stepped into the boat and held the flashlight for his father to get in.

Bert shoved the boat off and took up the oars. Kep sat in the bow with Bud snuggled against his legs. He would flash his light beam across the water ahead of the boat whenever his father needed it. The place where they were going to do their hunting was a mile ahead, where the slough they were now on met the river.

Bert methodically pulled his battered little craft through the darkness, and soon had covered the mile to the river. The first faint grayness of dawn was in the eastern sky as they left their boat.

Bud moved out into the brush, testing the autumn chill with his nose, and Kep followed his pa as he started up the slough bank. The thick-growing bull briers rattled against their clothes as they walked.

They had gone but a short distance when Bert signaled a halt and they stood with heads bent, listening. The excited pounding of Kep's heart was a thunder in his ear. Then he heard it: the murmuring, bustly, reedy sound of ducks!

"They'll be out of sight the other side of the water growth," Bert Lanning quietly told his son. "We'll cat-foot along and come up from behind."

Kep's pulse was racing so that it was making him, right here on a cool morning, wish for a drink of water. He loved his pa. He loved him for all that he had been to him in the past and for all that he would be to him in the future. But most of all, he loved him for this morning, this moment, this bringing him here, this standing shoulder to shoulder in the wash of dawn, hunting together.

They moved forward cautiously, came to the river, and slid down the bank onto a sand flat. Now only a screen of willows and reed growth lay between them and the murmuring ducks. They sat down on the sand. Pearly light was showing above the black panel of the forest on the east side of the river now, though the water itself was still in night. To the south Kep could see momentary flashes of light from the airport beacon ten miles away.

They waited there as silently as the river and the swamp, watching the day arrive. And it was a fine thing to see, as light the color of a dying campfire built up in the east. Finally the black shadows of earth began to melt, and gray-trunked trees came out of hiding.

The chatter of the ducks became more excited, then suddenly from beyond the screen of reeds they rose into the air. The whistling beat of their wings was like a sudden gust of wind blowing straight up into the sky. Their stout wings carried them up and up, then they wheeled and circled away for a taste of the new day.

Kep's pa said in a half-whisper, "They'll be back after they stretch their wings. Take it easy."

Daylight had spread over the woodland when they saw the ducks coming back. They came as a far-off

13

dangling sprig against the sky, twisting as though in a breeze. Then moments later they were close enough that their excited clacking could be heard.

Kep and his pa plunked shells into their guns and the breeches clicked shut together. Kep had to thumb his safety on because it wasn't working right and didn't automatically go on with the closing of the breech. Bud stood in a shivering, excited half-crouch, his belly almost touching the sand.

"When they start to settle," Bert whispered.

Kep nodded.

On the birds came, their wings drumming the air. As they spiraled downward, Bert Lanning said softly, "Now, son."

The dawn shattered as the two shotguns exploded, and the echo clattered against the woodland silence. Kep and his pa leaped to their feet and fired again. Three, four, five plump bodies with ragged wings plummeted out of the high dawn.

Kep stood with feet spread, gripping his gun, bony face lifted, charged with the heritage of all his ancestral hunters before him. Then, when the excitement of it reached his legs, they began to tremble.

In his mild, studied manner, Bert broke his gun, ejected the empties and stood the gun against a willow. Kep

14

did the same, his chest bursting with the joy of success and every muscle of his lank young body aching for even more excitement.

Bud proudly brought the birds in, one at a time, and didn't stop until all of them were on the sand at the water's edge.

"Boy, oh boy! Is he a retriever!" Kep shrieked, then tried hard to contain himself, wanting desperately to appear man-casual in his father's eyes.

"He done right good," Bert admitted. "We'd best get back to the blind. Could be another flock will come over and give us a chance at another shot."

They hurried toward their blind, and when they got there both reloaded and waited. Another small flock came in and they got two out of nine, then reloaded and waited again. At the end of another half-hour Bert said they might as well go on back to the boat.

"Be no more shootin' this mornin'," he said. "Sun's too high." He broke his gun and took out the shells and handed the gun to Kep to carry. Then he searched his overalls' pockets and found a piece of twine that he looped around the necks of the birds Bud had brought in. They started for the boat, Kep carrying the breech-broken guns and leading the way through the brush.

"How about him now?" he said to his pa as Bud

scurried past them. "Is he a good retriever or ain't he?"

" 'Bout as good as I ever seen work for a young dog," Bert Lanning admitted.

"He ought to be worth fifteen dollars, all right, hadn't he?" Kep asked, then not waiting for an answer, "I'm going to get the money to buy him some way, I'll tell you that."

They came to their rowboat and Kep stood the guns in, butts down, and leaned them against the mid-thwart. Bud leaped in, shook himself and jumped up onto the bow seat.

"I'll shove her out of the mud," Kep said to his pa, who was standing beside the boat, the string of ducks in his hand.

As Kep went toward the prow, he suddenly had the feeling that he had forgotten something. He tried to think what it could be. He patted his pockets but knew he hadn't taken his knife or anything out back there.

He bent over, placed both hands on the prow of the boat and gave a quick shove to free it from the mud bank. He gave just that one shove and the guns slid along the mid-thwart and struck the side of the boat. The breech of Kep's gun snapped shut and at that instant he knew what it was he had forgotten. He hadn't taken the shells out of his gun and hadn't thumbed the safety on.

As the gun struck the side of the boat one barrel exploded. The sound of it went rumbling and rocketing away in all directions. Kep was still bent over with his hands on the prow but out of the corner of his eye he saw the splash of fire and felt the boat shiver under the recoil.

The string of ducks slid from his pa's hand, slid down his leg and piled up in a mound of bloody feathers at the edge of the slough water. Some of them lay in the water. His pa bent over with a long groaning sound, then knelt down with both hands gripping his middle. Supported on his knees, he bent forward until his head touched the ground. He stayed like that for what seemed to Kep an eternity, then tumbled sideways. Kep saw the blood then. He saw his pa's eyes close, come halfway open, then close again slowly. But not closing entirely. Staying open a slit. Then he saw the eyes die behind the lids and the mind die behind the eyes.

chapter two

KEP ALONE

In the first moment Kep felt no shock, no surprise. He realized that he should never have leaned the guns against the thwart; he knew better than to do a thing like that. He should have seen that they were unloaded and the safeties on. You can't be too careful with a gun, son, his pa had always said.

Then the shock of it hit him. It seemed to strike first in his mind and spread through his body in waves, like tossing a pebble into still water, only a lot slower. Why didn't it hurry? Why didn't it hurt him? He sucked in his breath and set his teeth, trying to keep the horror away.

He told himself soberly that he mustn't go getting all flustered. No getting excited and going to pieces now. He knew better than that. And to prove that he knew

18

better he calmly stepped over and picked up his gun. He broke it and took both shells out and tossed the dead one into the bayou.

Then suddenly he was choking. A sickening sensation mixed with a desperate need to hurry was twisting at his throat, choking him. He knelt by his pa and wanted to talk to him, but even as he did he knew that his father was gone. And he knew whose fault it was. But he didn't need to talk to his pa about that; his pa already knew whose fault it was.

He slipped an arm under his father's shoulders. Best thing would be to put him in the boat. No, the first-aid lessons had said you don't move them. But what was it you were supposed to do? He couldn't remember that part of it. He closed his eyes, pinched them tight shut, trying to remember that part of it.

When he opened his eyes he was crying. Now there was reality. Now for the first time he seemed to be aware of what had happened and just how it had happened. He knelt there staring, not at the bloody abdomen, but at the face that was now turning gray. He kept shaking his head from side to side as if he were in great physical pain. His own voice was there, out there away from him somewhere saying, "No! No! No!" He wiped his hands on his Mackinaw, wanting to wipe all of it away, wanting to free himself of it.

19

A retching sob broke through his shock and for a moment he went all to pieces, beating his thighs with his fists and wailing and sobbing and shaking his head.

Finally he stopped crying, and stepped into the boat and took up the oars. Bud was still there on the bow seat. Kep shoved away from the muddy shore and set his oars and headed back up the bayou the way they had come. He kept his eyes averted from the still figure on the bank.

It seemed to take him a lot longer to cover the distance between the hunting place and home than it had taken them this morning. But he finally got there, tied his boat up, then ran as hard as he could to the shack where he and his pa had lived ever since his mother's death.

He ran up onto the porch and started to go inside. Then it came to him that he must go to town, to the sheriff's office, and tell what had happened. He quickly knelt down beside Bud and put an arm around him and told him he must stay here. As he did, it came to him painfully that here was the only creature in all the world that he now had to love. For a moment he put his face against the dog's silky hide. He hugged Bud, then again told him to stay, and ran down from the porch and toward town. He glanced back a couple of times to make sure Bud was staying at the house, then ran on in fear—terrible, hot, choking fear.

The North Florida town, though a county seat, was little more than a hamlet, set in a drab and stunted region of sawmills, small-acreage farms, brush and bogs. In the center of town stood the red-brick county courthouse, dusty and quiet in the mid-morning sun.

Kep was out of breath when he reached the main street so he slowed to a fast walk. When he came to the courthouse, he ran up the steps and into a dingy hall. He found a door marked SHERIFF, pushed it open and went in.

The sheriff was a big man with a gray mustache and heavy jowls. He was sitting behind a battered desk near a window, half asleep. Kep, in his anguish, almost ran across the room to the desk. He stopped in front of it and tried to speak. He couldn't make a sound. He gulped frantically, striving to make words come, while the sheriff blinked at him in puzzlement.

"What is it, boy?" the big man finally asked.

Kep blurted, "I did it! I shot my pa! I did it! I didn't mean to!"

The sheriff leaned forward. "What are you talkin' about, kid?"

Kep tried to tell the man all that had happened but

21

again his throat tightened up and he couldn't make a sound.

The sheriff motioned him to a chair then got heavily to his feet. He came around to the front of the desk, threw one barrel of a leg over the corner of it and looked at Kep. He laced his thick fingers together and began rubbing his thumbs against each other, while Kep waited with a sensation like drops of ice water trickling down through the hollowness of his body.

"What's your name?" the sheriff finally asked.

Every muscle of Kep's body jumped. He knew the big man had spoken in a normal tone, yet the voice seemed to fill the high-ceilinged room like an explosion.

"Kep Lanning," he managed to say. He heard the flatness of his own voice, heard the two words go drifting away like soap bubbles.

"Tell me all about what happened," the sheriff said.

Kep was nervously ramming his hands into his jacket pockets and taking them out again. He felt an icy drop of perspiration run down his neck from behind his right ear.

The sheriff sat patiently rubbing his thumbs together. "Tell me what happened, son," he said again.

Kep brought up a trembling hand and wiped it across his dry lips. That was the first he knew that his lips were quivering. He tried three times to speak and finally heard his voice come out in a kind of croak. But he didn't know what he said. He kept on talking, it seemed, but still didn't know what he was saying.

It seemed to him that a considerable period of time passed as he talked, though he couldn't be sure, for he felt as if he were in a sort of trance. All he knew for sure was that after a while the sheriff said, "That's all."

Kep blinked at him, wondering if the questioning was over. Had he answered all the man's questions? Had he told everything that happened?

He supposed that he must have, for the sheriff said again, "That's all. You can go."

Kep felt his face try to smile and wondered what there was to smile about. Then he remembered that his ma always said that a smile was a mark of politeness. His ma had set a heap of store by politeness.

Kep went out of the room and down the hall and outside and down the worn steps to the sidewalk. He walked slowly at first, his legs seeming very heavy. Then something like panic seized him suddenly and he ran until he came to the end of Main Street, where the sidewalk ended and a weed-grown path began. He had walked along here a thousand times. But everything seemed different now . . . changed somehow. It was like looking at everything from off in another world.

He came to where the path passed among the pine

trees, a favorite spot. But no picking up pine cones to throw now, no stopping to watch the ants racing up and down the rough bark of the trees as he had done so many times before. No pleasure in anything now. No pleasure ever again in all of his life.

He came to Mrs. Ames' house and walked fast past the picket fence he had painted for her last spring. Then, beyond her house, he came to his two-room shack home and sat down on the six-by-six front porch. His pa had built that porch from scraps he had brought from the sawmill on his shoulder.

Bud came around the house and up onto the porch and lay down beside him. Kep's hand unconsciously found one of the long soft ears. He bent over and again put his face against the dog's silken fur. When he sat up and put his back against the wall, Bud climbed onto his lap. He held the dog tight against his chest. Sitting there, his gaze reaching out across the roof of the swamp, he thought of his ma, and a sudden and terrible yearning to talk to her swept over him. He forced himself to think of something else.

He sat there until noon and on through the afternoon, the spaniel dozing in his arms. He sat there until the swamp trees softened in outline and receded into the blue haze of twilight that came seeping up out of the jungle depths. The spaniel became restless and wandered off, but Kep didn't move. He watched the last light of the sun spew its colors over the low hills beyond the town, watched the yellowish hue that moved up the sky to blend with the grayness overhead.

That was when it became clear to him that his pa was really gone. Until then it had seemed like only a bad dream. He clasped both hands around his knees and rocked back and forth, trying not to think, trying not to breathe, because even breathing seemed to make the pain of sadness worse.

In the next moment his lungs grabbed a deep gulp of air and a strangled sob burst from him. He fell over on the porch floor and lay face down. The spaniel came and stood over him, licking his ears and the back of his neck.

As he sprawled there, everything good and safe and beautiful seemed gone from Kep Lanning's life. He lay with his arms out and his fingers splayed, his cheek flat against the unplaned boards. His body shook with fear and pain and sorrow and the galling loneliness of being what he was, a human being.

After a while the spaniel growled softly and Kep sat up. In the heavy twilight he could see a white blur moving along the front path. It stopped at the gate, and he saw now that it was Mrs. Ames.

"Kep," she said softly.

25

He got to his feet and stepped down from the porch and went out to the front gate, the spaniel at his heels.

"Yes, Mrs. Ames?"

"Kep, why don't you come over and stay at my house tonight? Have you had any supper?"

He knew then that she had heard about it. "No, ma'am," he said politely. "I'm not hungry." He didn't want to be around anyone, didn't want to be asked any questions about it, didn't want anybody pitying him.

"You'd better come over to my house and stay," she said again. "I've got three or four rooms I don't use."

"I'm obliged to you, Mrs. Ames, but I ... well, I'll just stay here."

She peered at him through the twilight, a thin, small-ish, kindly woman. But he didn't like the pity in her voice and her staring at him like that. He didn't want any of it. He wished she hadn't come.

"Well, if you want to come and make it your home," she said, "I'll find plenty of after-school work for you so's you can earn your keep."

"I don't know. I'll study about it."

She was being kind and he knew he should be appreciative, but he couldn't feel appreciative. He didn't want anyone doing anything for him, because he knew they would just be feeling sorry for him.

As Mrs. Ames went back down the path, Kep crossed

his arms on the gatepost and stared off into the blackness that was the swamp where he and his pa had walked down the path together before daylight just this morning. His mouth drew in and he clamped his teeth over his lower lip to keep it from trembling. He put his head down on his crossed arms and stood there for a long time.

Finally he turned and went back up onto the porch and into the house. He walked down the breezeway that divided the house and went into the room they used as a kitchen and dining room. He lit a kerosene lamp and, using it to light his way, crossed the breezeway and went into the other room.

This room contained two canvas cots and three pieces of make-do furniture that his pa had made. On the walls were Kep's school drawings that Bert Lanning had always said were as good as any regular artist could do. He put the lamp on the upended orange crate that stood between the two cots. Then he undressed hurriedly, not looking at the cot that was his pa's. As he blew out the lamp and got into bed, he realized that Bud was there. He snapped his fingers and the dog leaped up onto the foot of the cot.

chapter three

A NEW PROSPECT

The day following the funeral Kep was sitting on his front porch in mid-afternoon when he saw a car coming. As it came closer, he recognized the driver. It was Preacher Barton of the church where he and his pa went, and who had read the service at Bert Lanning's funeral.

Preacher Barton was smiling in friendliness as he stopped his car at Kep's gate and got out and came toward the porch.

"Hello, Kep," he greeted.

Kep made no move, said nothing, but merely nodded a greeting. He knew instinctively that the preacher had come to talk to him. And he wondered what the talk was to be about.

The preacher sat down on the low porch and rested one foot on the bottom step. Bud came around the house, saw the stranger and wiggled up to him for a greeting.

"Well, hello there!" the preacher said. He bent over and took one silky ear in his hand. "What's his name?"

"Bud. He ain't mine. I just borrowed him."

"Oh."

"He belongs to Mr. Smath." As he said it he turned a dull gaze on the minister. "Did you come to ask me about it ... about what happened to my pa? Everybody keeps wanting me to tell them about it. Are you fixing to make me tell it to you?"

The minister looked deep into the stricken brown eyes, studied the tragic young face. He knew that if there was ever a human being who needed love and kindness it was this boy.

"No, Kep," he said. "I didn't come here to try to get you to tell me anything. In fact I came to tell you something." He stood up then and gave all of his attention to the dog. "Come here, boy!" He walked out into the yard and picked up a stick. "Here, Bud! Get it!" He threw the stick.

Kep watched the two of them playing, the tall gangly man chasing the dog, and throwing the stick for him. Once Bud, the stick clamped in his jaws, dodged sud-

denly and the preacher almost fell down. Kep laughed
without knowing he was going to do it. And when he
laughed, something seemed to jar loose inside of him,
something cold and paralyzing. He felt better.

After ten minutes of play, the preacher threw the
stick one last time, then came over and again sat on the
porch, panting.

"Winds me more than playing baseball with the kids
in my Sunday School class," he grinned. Then after a
moment he said, "No, Kep, like I said, I didn't come to
ask you anything. I came to tell you about a boy."

"What boy?" Kep asked suspiciously.

"Someone you don't know. Oh, by the way, I was
talking to your school principal the other day."

"I ain't going back to school!" Kep said quickly, irri-
tably, prepared for an argument.

The preacher ignored the sharpness in his tone.
"Your principal and I were talking about that very
thing, and he said he wasn't in favor of your coming
back right away. That is, unless you just wanted to."

"I don't want to."

The preacher bent over and stripped a long sliver
from the porch step. He sat breaking the sliver into tiny
bits and letting them fall as he talked. Bud sat on his
haunches with his head tipped to one side and interestedly watched each tiny bit of wood that fell.

30

"Your principal was telling me about your drawing, Kep. He said you make some nice drawings."

Kep said nothing.

"He also said you're a good ball player, a good pitcher. Is that right?"

Kep was looking off toward the swamp, his fingers laced around his knees. "Plenty of kids in school are better than me."

"Well, the principal says you're one of the best in your class. Anyway, it's partly about baseball that I came to talk to you."

Kep glanced at him, then away.

"I used to play some ball when I was in high school," the preacher said. He reached down and patted Bud's head. "Pitched some. I wasn't so hot." Again he gave his attention to the spaniel, then finally straightened up and looked steadily at Kep. "Kep, if a guy who was really a regular fellow had something happen to him and needed, really needed, someone to go to bat for him, would you step up and try to smash one out to center field for him? You know, if he badly needed someone to pinch hit for him?"

Kep's eyes searched the preacher's smiling face. "What is this you're getting at?"

"I was just wondering if you'd do that."

"I don't know. I'd have to study about it."

The preacher now laced his own fingers around one knee and looked at Kep. "I know of a boy who needs someone to go to bat for him."

"What boy?"

"This boy I came to talk to you about. Jimmy Maskew was his name."

"Was his name?"

"Yes. He used to live about three or four hundred miles from here, over in Pine Valley, Mississippi."

"Where does he live now?"

"He's dead."

Kep's lips compressed into a tight line. He snapped his head half around and looked away.

"Jimmy's mother has been in pretty bad shape since he's gone," the preacher went on, talking slowly, casually. "He died of polio. He's gone, but someone ought to go to bat for him. I mean, the mother and father need someone to take Jimmy's place. Especially the mother does. You see, for a long time I've known a minister near the town where Jimmy lived and he had written me about the father and mother. It occurred to me that you might like to help them. So I talked to my friend on the phone and also to Jimmy's father. His name is Chester Maskew. He wants you to come and live with them, Kep."

Kep flushed angrily. "I don't want nobody taking pity

on me!" Then he stole a cautious glance at the preacher. The man seemed sincere, seemed to want to help him.

"I can understand your not wanting to be pitied," the preacher said. "But it would be a good thing, Kep. You'd be doing a wonderful thing for those parents. You see, something bad may happen to Jimmy's mother if she isn't helped. Something might happen to her mind. If it was the other way around, if it was your mother, wouldn't you want some guy to go to bat for you? Wouldn't you appreciate that?"

"I don't know. I reckon so."

"Wouldn't you be willing to go there and be a son to Jimmy's parents?"

Kep looked up from studying his thumbnails. He moved his gaze across the western sky where the sun was spreading its light along the top of some dark clouds.

The preacher said, "Don't try to decide right now, Kep. It would be best if you thought on it for a while. You can let me know." He stood up. Kep stood up too, and the preacher put an arm about his shoulders as they walked toward the gate.

"Do you know what preachers are for, Kep?"

Kep pondered that. "To help folks, my ma always said. To teach folks how to be good."

"Well, that's right. But more than that, a preacher's

mission is to help folks understand the importance of helping others. So you think this over, and if you decide to go, Mr. Maskew will wire me the money for your train fare."

"But I wouldn't want to be owing anybody anything."

The minister smiled and gave the shoulder under his hand a friendly pat. "You wouldn't be owing anything. Mr. Maskew would adopt you. You'd be his son. You'd carry on for Jimmy. It would be like—well, like if you were away at school and your father sent you money to come home for the Christmas holidays. You wouldn't be owing the money."

The minister went to his car then. He got in, lifted a hand to Kep and drove away.

Kep watched him go, then stood with his arms crossed on the gatepost, looking toward the swamp. Now he must decide what to do. Why had the preacher come here? Why did he have to say all that and bring up another problem that had to be decided? Why were things always coming up to make you have to decide something, when you never knew which way to decide?

Suddenly he turned and ran down the path toward the swamp, as hard as he could go. Bud was right behind him.

He ran hard until he came to where the bushes grew

heavy along both sides of the path, and they slowed him. Pushing through he hurried on until he came to a favorite old log, where he sat down. But the familiar spot didn't help. Looking around him, it seemed that even the woods didn't like him any more. It seemed that even the tops of the trees swaying in the breeze were trying to confuse him, to mix him up worse than he was. It was as if they were nodding to him, telling him he simply had to decide what he wanted to do. Even Bud was no help, for he had gone off into the brush to sniff around.

Kep tried to think over all that the preacher had said. He just didn't know what he wanted to do about going to live with Jimmy Maskew's parents. In a way it would be a good thing, not only for Jimmy's mother but for himself. He'd have a home again, and a ma and pa to love him, even if they weren't his real ones. Besides, in that town no one would know what he had done to his pa. Maybe that would help him get rid of the awful jumps that he'd had inside of him ever since the accident happened. 2080690

Bud came out of the brush and sat down by him. Kep slid from the log to the ground and put an arm around the spaniel. Now that at last he had a dog to love, he was going to have to give him up, if he went to live with the Maskews. That was making it harder to decide what to do. He hadn't had many pets in his life, and never

35

one that loved him as the spaniel did. He didn't know how he could ever have gotten through the ordeal of the tragedy if it hadn't been for Bud. That hurting thing inside him of having to decide what to do seemed to grow larger. He put his forehead down on Bud and almost let the tears come, but didn't.

Kep sat a long time with his arm about the spaniel, feeling the breeze that had sprung up with the approach of evening. He watched the swaying of some slender vines high in the top of a gum tree, and fought the sickness that was in him because of having to part with Bud. For he had made up his mind that he was going to live with the Maskews.

He spent a half-hour concentrating on picking beggar lice out of Bud's shiny coat. Then abruptly he stood up, buttoned his jacket and spoke to Bud.

"It's time to go, boy," he told the dog. "I got to take you back. I'll talk to him about keeping you, but likely it won't do any good, because I ain't got any money at all. But I'll talk to him."

They started back the way they had come.

A hundred yards below his shack Kep took a path that led around the head of the swamp and to the south side of town. After ten minutes of walking they came to a high fence with vines growing so thick over it that it was like a green wall. Kep put his hand on the gate, a

36

heavy, sagging structure, and swung it open and went through. Set back, in a huge front yard that looked like a hayfield, was the unpainted house where Sam Smath lived with his hunting dogs. A half-dozen hounds and some mixed-breeds came blaring through the twilight and Kep stopped to pet all of them, calling them by their names, then went on to the house.

Sam Smath was standing on his front porch in a slouched stance, one beefy shoulder pressed against an upright. He was picking his teeth with a pocketknife.

"Hi, bub," he greeted Kep jovially.

Kep indicated Bud and said, "I brought him back, Mr. Smath." Suddenly he was afraid this man, like others, was going to ask him how he happened to shoot his pa. Thinking that, his palms dampened and his legs began to tremble.

"Brought him back, huh?" Sam Smath rumbled. He snapped his pocketknife shut and put it in his pocket, then wiped supper grease from his stubbled chin with the back of his hand.

"Yes, sir. I wanted to buy him but—I can't," Kep said. "You see, I'm—I'm going away."

"Oh?"

"Up to Mississippi." He kicked at the damp ground with the toe of his sneaker. "I'd still like to have him, though. He's a fine dog, all right. Don't reckon you'd

37

want to let me take him along with me, then send the money back to you?"

Sam Smath sucked his teeth noisily. "Reckon not, boy. Done had a feller here ready to pay me cash for a good retriever."

"Yes, sir. Well, then I reckon you'd want to sell Bud to him. And that'd likely be best for Bud too. He'd get plenty of hunting. I'd want him to have that."

Kep knelt by the spaniel and said good-bye in the dog and boy way that no one in the world but the two of them ever understands. No spoken words. Just sounds. Sounds that anyone could see the dog understood. The young hands gently stroking the sturdy back, caressing the silken ears. Then the head bending over and the cheek against the smooth head. A whispered word, a moist tongue for reply, and it was said.

Kep stood up, thanked the dark-jawed man on the porch for the use of the dog and walked away into the cool twilight. A high-shouldered boy in worn jacket and shapeless cap, lonely, with nothing for company now but the sadness and the fear and the confusion of the past days drawing down on him, closing in. Behind him, by the porch steps, was all that was left of the good life he had known.

chapter four

MEETING THE MASKEWS

Kep went to Preacher Barton the next day and told him that he had decided the best thing would be to go live with the Maskews in Mississippi. The preacher was pleased, and told him he would phone the Maskews, then pick him up very early the next morning and take him to the train.

By daylight Kep was on his way to his new home. It took almost the entire day to make the trip, and it was nearing evening when the conductor called Pine Valley.

A tightness of expectancy rose in Kep at the sound of the name of the town. Now he would see his new parents, his new home, the town where he would probably live the rest of his life. It was like being born again. But there was a feeling of uncertainty in him about these new people. Would they like him? Would he like them? After he met them would he be glad or sorry that he had come here? If he was sorry, what could he do about it?

When the train began to slow down he took his suitcase from the overhead rack and walked down the aisle, looking out the windows for a sight of the town. It had been misting rain for two hours and he couldn't see very much. By the time the town did come into view, the train was almost stopped; that's how small the place was. But he was glad of that because he didn't think he would have felt at home in a big town.

He stepped off the train into the misty drizzle, the only passenger to get off. He put his suitcase down, buttoned his Mackinaw, and pulled his cap down tight on his head.

Tiny drops of mist formed on his eyelashes as he watched the tan Buick turn off the street to the south and come toward the station. As the car stopped at the end of the platform, he decided the driver must be Chester Maskew. He was wearing a gray raincoat and his hat brim was turned down, half shielding his face. He got out and came along the platform.

"I suppose you're Kep," he said with a friendly smile, putting out his hand.

"Yes, sir," Kep said. He took the hand timidly.

"I'm glad you got here all right," Chester said, and

laughed in a nervous, pleased way. "I guess we'd better get in the car out of this wet."

He offered to carry Kep's suitcase but Kep said he'd take it, and they walked together through the drizzle to the waiting car, the boy almost as tall as the man.

Kep had never before been in such a luxurious car, and he felt ashamed sitting on the broad nylon-covered seat in his worn and faded jeans and threadbare Mackinaw with sleeves that struck him two inches above the wrist bones.

"I'm glad you decided to come, Kep," Chester said as he backed the car away from the platform and swung around. "We're going to be mighty happy, having you with us, and I hope you'll be happy, too."

Kep already liked this slender, timidly smiling man who was going to be his pa. He liked the gentleness of his voice and the friendliness of his pale blue eyes.

"My wife is not at home," Chester told him. "She went to Jackson to visit her sister, and there'll be just you and me at the house for a few days. We don't have a cook; used to have a woman who lived with us, but since our son's death it seems to make my wife sort of nervous to have another woman around. But there's plenty of stuff at home to eat, so I guess we can make out, eh? What would you like for supper?"

"It don't matter," Kep said. "I ain't very hungry."

41

"Well, we'll see what we can throw together."

Chester drove around the town square pointing out the business establishments to Kep: a department store, barber shop, dress shop, grocery, movie theatre, the usual business of a small town.

"There's my newspaper office," he said, pointing to a brick building.

"Newspaper?" Kep asked.

"Yes, I print the only paper in town. I established it a good many years ago."

Kep didn't miss the faint note of pride in his tone.

"It's a nice town, all right," Kep said.

"We here think it is," Chester answered, the pride in his voice a little stronger. "County seat, as you can see." He tipped his head at the courthouse in the center of the square. "We try to keep it up to what a county seat ought to be."

Chester was feeling at ease now, telling about his town and what his newspaper had achieved for the town over the years. As he talked he was observing the clean line of Kep's jaw and the frank expression of his soft brown eyes. And he was thinking, *There's a lot of good in this lad. I'm glad I sent for him; he and Oda will be good for each other.*

Now Chester drove up Jackson Street. As he turned into his private road, Kep saw that there was only one house the graveled road could lead to. He sat staring at the long, low brick house, unable to believe that he was going to live in such a fine place.

A front porch ran the entire length of the building. The garage was of matching red brick and there was a small white frame building at the rear of the garage that Kep guessed would be a workshop. The yard was fenced, and there was a curving driveway, with a concrete walk leading up to the porch. Kep took note of the shrubbery, the mulberry and chinaberry trees along the south side of the yard, the vegetable garden plot beyond the south fence. He couldn't ever remember having seen a nicer place in his life.

When Chester drove into the garage they got out and went up on the long porch. Chester unlocked the door and told Kep to go in.

"I'll show you your room," he said as he stepped in behind Kep and closed the door. "I suppose you'll want to wash up a bit. While you're doing that I'll see what I can find in the kitchen to cook."

As he stood there just inside the door, with his cap in one hand and his suitcase in the other, Kep supposed that there were probably better houses than this somewhere in the world, but he doubted it. The long living room, two steps down, was floored with boards so narrow that his pa would have called them pales. They were highly polished, as were the steps going down, and there was a shaggy tan rug on the floor. The living room was paneled in some sort of wood that was the color of yellow corn stalks. All the furniture in the room was big and inviting, and there were some real nice paintings on the walls that he wanted to examine later.

He had thought when he saw the outside of the house that he would feel out of place here, but he didn't. It was the finest house he had ever been in, but it somehow made him feel at home and welcome. He thought how strange it was that a house could do that.

He followed Chester across the living room and up two steps again to the hall, which was thickly carpeted. They walked down it with Chester turning on lights as they went.

"The house is a bit chilly," he said; "needs a little heat. We have gas. There's a small heater in your room." He stopped at a door and said, "This is where you'll sleep," and pushed the door open.

Kep stepped into the room and looked about, speechless. He was wondering what it was going to be like to sleep in a bed with a mattress as thick as the one on the maple bed.

"You make yourself at home," Chester said. "There's a bath right next to your room. I'll go get something started cooking."

44

Left alone, Kep still stood looking around the room, unable to convince himself that he was really going to live here. The walls of the room were of knotty pine and the ceiling was rough tan plaster. There were some pictures around the room, mostly of dogs, and on one wall were three china birds arranged so they appeared to be in flight. There was a bookcase with a golden horse on it, and above, on the wall, a half dozen pennants. A baseball bat was standing in one corner, and in the center of the room, up near the ceiling, a model airplane hung on hair-thin wire to look as if it were flying. Lying across the bed was a fresh pair of pajamas.

Standing there in the room that he knew had been Jimmy Maskew's with Jimmy's things about him, Kep was genuinely glad he had come here. Preacher Barton had been right: It was truly a good thing to be able to go to bat for the other fellow.

Besides, he was going to like it here, he was sure of that. Already he liked Chester. Of course, he'd kind of have to get used to these people. He had never known anyone like Chester before. But then, he had never known anybody as rich as the Maskews seemed to be. That was probably why Chester seemed sort of different from other men he had known, men like his pa and the other sawmill hands his pa had worked with.

He wondered what Mrs. Maskew would be like.

45

Something like Chester, probably—kind of different. Not like his ma and Mrs. Ames and women like that. Being a rich man's wife, she'd most likely be different, all right. She would be pleasant enough, the same as Chester was, and treat him nice, but would she like him?

He wondered why she had gone to Jackson to visit her sister when she had a new boy coming to take her son's place. Well, maybe her sister had taken sick all of a sudden or something like that. Maybe she had intended to be back before now; Chester hadn't said.

By the time Kep was cleaned up and ready for supper it was almost dark outside. He turned the light out in his room and went to the dinette. He could smell sausage cooking the moment he opened the door.

"You're just in time," Chester said. "Did you find towels and soap?"

"Yes, sir. Golly, Mr. Maskew, you got a sure-'nough fine house. And you know...I feel at home here already."

"Well, I'm glad to hear that," Chester said, pleased. "I want you to consider it your home right off."

"Much obliged."

"How about hotcakes, you like them?"

"Pancakes? Yeh, I sure do," Kep said. He couldn't get over how much at home he felt here already. It was hard to believe that he had known Chester only about an hour.

"We've got to think about your schooling, Kep," Chester said as he put a platter of hotcakes on the table. "What grade are you in?"

"Tenth."

"Good. Well, sit down and let's get started on those flapjacks." When they were seated, Chester said casually, "I've been thinking that we'd go downtown in the morning and buy you some school clothes."

Kep dropped his eyes to his plate in embarrassment. "I reckon so. I sure ain't got no clothes much."

"That's fine," Chester said pleasantly. "I'm glad to hear that. I was sort of afraid you'd come here with plenty of clothes—and well, I just feel that starting a new life here with us, you ought to start all new."

Kep knew that was Chester's way of sparing him embarrassment, and he was grateful. "Well, I reckon that would be best," he agreed.

"You'll start school right away," Chester told him. "I'll register you tomorrow. We'll get you squared away in no time, and you'll feel as if you've always lived here."

When they had finished eating, they washed the dishes together, then went to the living room, lighted the logs in the imitation fireplace and turned on the television set. They sat together on the big sofa and Kep became so engrossed in watching the performance that he couldn't believe it when Chester said it was ten o'clock and time to get to bed because they had a lot to do tomorrow.

They said good night and Kep went to his room. He took a hot bath and put on the pajamas that were on the bed, then got into the softest bed he had ever lain on in his life. The wind had come up and the drizzle had turned to rain. He lay contentedly listening to the wind and the rain, scratching at the windows like a playful kitten. Soon the muffled sound of it lifted him out of his consciousness.

THE NEXT THING he knew there was a scream. A woman's scream. A wild piercing shriek that slashed across his sleep-dulled mind like a sharp blade. He was instantly sitting up in bed, frozen. The light was on. Standing in the doorway, one black-gloved hand on the light switch, was a white-faced woman with stark terror in her wide black eyes.

He got just that one glimpse of her, then the light went off, the door banged shut and he could hear her running down the hall, wailing and sobbing. A door closed heavily down there and a moment later anoth-

48

er one opened and he could hear Chester, hurrying along the hall in his bare feet. Then there was again the closing of a door. Outside, lightning flashed and bursts of thunder shook the earth. The wind and rain howled beyond the windows. The playful kitten had now become a snarling panther.

Kep sat with every muscle of his body stiff and frozen and aching. Ropes of fright tightened painfully inside of him, and it was impossible to clamp his teeth tight enough to keep them from chattering. But he lay back on the bed and finally the fright drained out of him.

He told himself there was nothing to be afraid of. The woman, of course, was Mrs. Maskew. She must have come home sooner than Chester had expected, otherwise he would have met her at the station. And when she turned on the light and saw someone in her son's bed, it naturally gave her a scare. It would any woman.

Kep wished she had come on in so he could have talked with her, the way his own ma used to come to his bed and talk to him sometimes before he went to sleep. He lay there for a while thinking Chester might bring her to the room, but he didn't. Kep wondered why. You'd think Chester would have wanted them to get acquainted right away. Maybe she was too badly scared to want to talk tonight.

Kep lay listening to the storm and thinking about Chester and his wife and wondering what she would be like. Then he began to wonder how it was going to be for him, living in a fine house like this, with people who had always been rich. What was it going to be like? What were all the years ahead going to be like for him?

After a while he again drifted off to sleep.

chapter five

PERSONALITY PROBLEMS

Chester Maskew was a light sleeper. If it
hadn't been for the storm he would have heard Gabe
Saunders' old taxi drive up, but he hadn't. Nor did the
sound of the motor and the scraping gears when Gabe
drove away awaken him. But his wife's scream and the
banging of the door to Kep's room did. He leaped out of
bed and got into his robe, wondering sleepily why in the
world he had put the boy in Jimmy's room anyway. Or
why hadn't he told Kep to lock his door?

He hurried down the hall to his wife's room where
she sat on the edge of a straight-backed chair in the
middle of the room, her dark raincoat dripping water
on the polished floor. Her elbows were on her knees and

her face was buried in her shaking hands. She looked up at him, black eyes horrified, bulging.

"I thought it was Jimmy!" she whimpered pitifully. "I thought . . ." Her voice broke off and she again buried her face in her hands.

Chester walked over to her and stood there helplessly, the floor cold beneath his bare feet. He stood looking down at her, a woman whose sorrow of a year ago had left her mercilessly stranded in a black world of agonizing confusion. He timidly put a hand on her wet, slightly graying hair.

"I'm sorry, Oda," he said. "I should have let you know I was bringing the boy here, but I was afraid if I told you I was sending for him, you'd object. I hope after you get to know him, he'll be a help to you. It seemed to me you'd be glad to have a son again, and that you would want me to put him in Jimmy's room. Of course, if I had known you were coming home in the middle of the night I would have told you about him. Then you wouldn't have been so startled."

Her silence caused him to wonder with apprehension what relationship she and Kep would have in the future. They needed each other, that he knew, and they could help each other a great deal, if they came to like each other. Kep was a good boy, anybody could see that. He would like Oda, but would Oda like him?

Now Chester said to his wife, "Oda, you must get ready for bed."

She said nothing. He felt helpless, alone, the way he felt most of the time in her presence now. Looking down on her slender heaving shoulders, he regretted causing her this fright. If only she could cry, he thought, really cry, it might give her some comfort in her sorrow over the loss of Jimmy.

"Oda, get your wet things off and go to bed," he urged.

She looked up at him with an expression of hurt surprise and failure to understand which gradually hardened on her face. She walked, shoulders very straight, to a window where she stood staring out into the stormy blackness. Not crying. Just whimpering like an injured animal.

Chester knew it was useless to try to comfort her. He had tried so many times before. He lit the gas in the fireplace and went to the kitchen to make coffee for her. She was still staring into the darkness when he put her coffee on the night table and began telling her all about Kep. She did not speak until he finished. Then she said, in a voice that was as tense as spun glass, "You'll have to send him back, Chester. He can't stay here."

He drew in a deep breath and tried not to speak to her as if she were an invalid. "No, Oda, I'm not going

to send him back. I plan to adopt him. You'll have to
get used to having him here. I—I had hoped you'd love
him. He is a boy who greatly needs love."

He went out softly and closed the door.

WHEN CHESTER came out of his bedroom the
next morning, his wife was nowhere to be seen. He
didn't call her because he knew plenty of rest was the
best thing for her. He did call Kep and went into the
kitchen. As he prepared breakfast he planned the day.
First he would take Kep to a clothing store and leave
him to be outfitted while he himself drove to the school.
He would explain to Kep's teachers the shock the boy
had experienced at the death of his father. The entire
community, Chester knew, would be happy to help this
boy whom he and Oda had taken in to ease the sorrow
of their own loss.

As Chester and Kep went out to the garage, they saw
that the rain had stopped. Now the world was wrapped
in soggy, dripping grayness, and the town at the foot of
the slope lay in chilly early-morning quiet. The roofs of
houses were rain blackened and the paved streets were
as shiny as spilled oil in the gray light.

They drove to town and Chester parked in front of
the town's only clothing store for men and boys.

54

"I guess we're the first customers this morning, eh, Arthur?" Chester greeted the proprietor. "We want some clothes. For Kep here." He introduced Kep to the storekeeper and said, "Here's a list I made out, Arthur. You fix him up. Ought to be about what he'll need there." He gave the man the list then said to Kep, "If there's anything I forgot just tell Arthur." He took his wallet from his pocket and handed Kep three dollars. "After you're through here, go to the barber shop and get yourself a haircut, then come on over to my office. I'm going up to the school to register you. Say, what about your report card?"

"Well, I—I didn't get it when I left school."

"No matter. We'll get that straightened out later."

After he attended to matters at the school, he returned to his office where he found Kep, dressed in a new outfit, his hair neatly cut.

"Fine, fine!" Chester said, looking him over.

Kep grinned. "I sort of feel like I'm not me."

"You look okay. The clothes are a good fit."

"All the others had to be altered some. I can pick them up tomorrow."

"Good!" Chester said, and took him behind a railing to introduce him to some people working in the newspaper office.

"How would you like to take a short drive up through

the hills?" Chester asked. "You can get a good view of valley and the town from up there."

"I'd like that," Kep said. "I never lived where there were any hills to speak of before."

They left the office, got into Chester's car and drove east on Jackson Street, past the road leading to his house. Soon they were grading up a long hill.

"You're registered in school," Chester said. "You'll start this afternoon. We'll go back to town for lunch."

Kep nodded.

Chester turned off on what he said was called the Ridge Road and headed south. They came to a clearing and he stopped the car.

"The town sits at the edge of a valley, as you can see," he said.

Kep looked down on the town and the vast spread of flat land beyond. "Say, this is a sight from up here! Sure can see a long way, can't you?"

"Yes, you can. The low hills off yonder are the west rim of the valley."

"The paved road goes straight across the valley, doesn't it?"

"Yes, and as you can see, the railroad comes down this side, then angles across."

"Your house is easy to pick out from up here."

"*Our* house," Chester smiled.

"Yeah, our house," said Kep with a grin. "That hill over there with the steep sides, what's that?"

"That's called Morton's Knob. There's a lake south of town too; you can see just a little of it from here."

"Any fish in it?"

"Yes, and there's trout in the creeks around here too." He started the car. "Ahead of us and to the east is hill country. They do a lot of fox and coon hunting up in here in the fall."

Autumn was stalking down all the slopes, robbing the trees and bushes of their greenery. Driving along, Kep and Chester would occasionally get a glimpse of a patch of brown pasture with ponds that shone like new dimes. Here and there small bunches of cattle were scattered over the flat lands.

"Some good hill farms all through here," Chester said.

"We used to live on a farm," Kep told him. "We called it a hill farm but ours weren't no hills at all compared to these." He glanced at Chester. "Have you always lived here?"

"No, Oda and I came to Pine Valley shortly after we were married, and I bought the newspaper."

Chester had noticed Kep's reaction to the things of nature such as the pond, the lake, and the hills. And his talk of fishing and hunting. He thought how little time he himself had given to such things over the years. He had been too busy to share and enjoy the outdoors with his own son and had completely forgotten how thrilling nature in all of its phases could be to a boy in his teens. To himself he admitted, *I seem to have forgotten how it is to be a boy. Or did I ever know? I don't think I ever did. My father never felt it was important for a boy to be a boy. He felt that a boy should think and work and plan for the time when he would be a man, and decide how he could build financial security for himself. Those things I learned well, but now I hardly know how to communicate with this boy. To understand him, I should be the kind of man who enjoys being a boy right along with him. I wanted to be that sort of father to my own son, but somehow I never could.*

When Chester turned the car around to go back home, he said to Kep, "About last night, Kep. I suppose you've guessed that my wife came home." He said it embarrassedly, watching the road ahead.

"Yes, sir."

"I'm afraid she frightened you. You see, she knew nothing about your being here. I wasn't expecting her home last night." There was an awkward pause before he said, "I must explain about her, Kep. She's not well. She's got what you might call a mental sickness. Oh, her mind is sound enough, it's just that she has never recovered from the shock of our son's death. It's a bad thing when people can't get over a shock like that. I'm sure that eventually she'll be all right. And I think you can help her a lot, just by being here with us."

"I hope I can," Kep said, staring off down the timbered slope.

"I think the very best thing for her is your being here. I think she needs someone to take our son's place," Chester went on. "Of course, it'll probably take a little time for her to get used to you." He smiled apologetically. "For that matter, I suppose it will take a while for you to get adjusted to her too. It won't be long, I'm sure, until the three of us will be a happy family. When we see that it's all going to work out okay, I'd like to adopt you. That is, if it's all right with you."

"Well—sure. I reckon so," Kep said. "I'm sure obliged to you, giving me a home and all."

"I just wanted to explain about Oda, so you'd understand her behavior. It was my fault that she was upset last night. I shouldn't have put you in Jimmy's room. You see, she doesn't want anything disturbed in there. There's a room at the end of the hall, a nice little room that the woman who used to cook and keep house for us had. If it's all right, that will be your room."

"Sure it's all right," Kep said. "Gosh, I'm pleasured just to have any room at all."

59

"We'll fix you up then. It'll be your very own room, where you can have all your own things just the way you want them."

"That'll be fine," Kep reassured him.

"Now you'll get two dollars a week allowance besides whatever you need in the way of clothes. And I'll give you extra money when you need it, though in a town this size there isn't much of any place to spend money. Maybe you'll want to go off when the school team plays away from home or something like that."

Kep stared at him. "Two dollars a week?"

"Yes, that's what Jimmy's allowance was."

"Why, you've already given me all these clothes! I don't need two dollars a week."

"You can use it," Chester smiled. "There'll be movies you'll want to see, a soda once in a while. Or you can save it, if you'd rather." Chester smiled at him. "It's going to be fine for Oda and me, having a boy in the house again. Really fine."

Even as he said it, Chester wondered if it was. For himself, yes, but how was it going to be for Oda? What was more important, how was it going to be for this boy? He glanced at Kep's thin face with its soft brown eyes and gentle, sensitive mouth. What was in his mind? Why had Kep been so noncommittal a few minutes ago when he had tried to talk to him about Oda's mental troubles and her strangeness?

chapter six

A BAD DAY

Chester drove back to town where he and Kep had lunch at a cafe on the square. Then he drove to the school, a one-story brick structure with a large playground area.

As he brought the car to a stop before the building, Chester said proudly, "It's one of the best schools around here, for the size of the town. We have lots of students come in from surrounding areas by school bus."

"Well, I'll see you after school," Kep said as he got out.

"Okay. You go to room nineteen, Miss Hammond's room."

"All right," Kep called back as he walked toward the school entrance. "See you."

Passing students on the grounds, Kep felt stiff and tense. He kept telling himself it was foolish to be afraid. All of these kids were strangers to him. Not one of them knew anything about him or his tragedy. He tried to bring his will power to a sharp focus on those facts by saying to himself, nobody here knows me. Nobody here knows me. Nobody here knows me.

When he found room nineteen it was already half filled with students and more were crowding in. He walked over to the teacher at her desk. She was a small-ish woman with a thin face and gray in her hair.

"Are you Miss Hammond?" Kep asked.

"Yes, I am."

"I'm Kep Lanning. I reckon Mr. Maskew told you about me."

Miss Hammond stood up. "Oh, the Lanning boy. Oh, yes, Mr. Maskew told me about you." She passed her kindly gaze over him. "I'm glad to have you in my class. You'll take the seventh seat back on the outside row there." He sat down in the seat she had pointed out.

When the class was in their seats, Kep could feel every eye in the room turn to him. With the eyes came that awful fear that as soon as classes were over, his schoolmates would be asking him to tell them how he killed his pa. He wiped his soggy palms on his trousers.

Miss Hammond, still standing beside her desk, got the attention of the class without saying a word, the way a teacher can, and when the room was quiet she said, "Class, we have a new student with us." Kep didn't take his eyes from her face. "This is Kep Lanning, the boy I told you about." A breath caught in Kep's throat and nearly choked him. "And remember," the teacher's thin voice went on, "as I told you this morning, tragedy could come to any one of you, just as it came to Kep." A hot, dry pain went stabbing through Kep, making him sick. "So I want all of you to be nice to Kep. Be friendly to him. The time may come when you too will need sympathy."

Kep sat there pushing his feet hard against the desk legs, pushing his back against the seat with all his strength. One sweaty hand, out of sight under the desk, was trying to pull the fingers of the other loose from their sockets.

To himself he was fairly shouting, *They know. They all know. She told them. Chester told her and she told them. Every kid in the whole school will know about it by tomorrow.*

He wasn't going to let it bother him. He kept telling himself, *I won't let it bother me. I won't.* But he couldn't stop that awful scared shaking that was inside of him; couldn't stop sweating and feeling cold at the same time.

The teacher was saying something to him. He forced himself to listen to her.

"—and you will go with the others to room nine for history."

A bell rang somewhere, and a dozen or more students stood up and filed out. Kep went with them. He walked behind the others down a long hall. When they turned into room nine Kep kept going. He walked out an open door at the end of the hall, crossed the school grounds and went toward town.

As he walked along he wondered what he would do now. He couldn't go back to school. He wouldn't go back! Not with every kid in school knowing that he killed his pa. He couldn't go home, not this time of day. How would he ever be able to tell Chester?

If it were his own pa he would know how to tell him. Because his own pa was always understanding whenever there was trouble to be dealt with. That was probably because he himself had had to meet up with and handle so many troubles during his lifetime.

Kep didn't know whether Chester would be able to understand a thing like this or not, because he didn't yet know Chester very well. He liked him. He wanted to know him well enough to be sure how he would be whenever something bad like this came along. But how

64

could he understand Chester, whom he had met so recently, the way he had understood his own pa?

Kep began to run. It always helped, it seemed, to run whenever he had bad troubles. He came to the town square, to the movie house, where a sign at the box office said there was a matinee today. He bought a ticket and went in.

When he came out, there were kids on the street so he knew school was out. He went home, and as he walked up the front walk, he heard some hammering in the little white frame building at the rear of the garage. As he had supposed, the building was a workshop. Chester was there, busy at his workbench.

"Hi," he said as Kep appeared at the door. "How was school?"

"All right," Kep said casually.

"Good! I thought I'd do a little work out here. Haven't been in here for a long time. I've been planning on making a barbecue pit in the back yard. Be fun, don't you think, cooking supper outdoors sometimes, barbecuing ribs and such?"

"Yeah," Kep said, and stepped over to a bicycle standing by the door. He took hold of the handlebars and swung them back and forth. He felt the tires.

"You ride a bike?" Chester asked absently.

"Some. I never owned one, but a kid I knew let me ride his sometimes." He spun one of the pedals with his toe.

"Go ahead and ride it," Chester said. He was studying a drawing of his proposed barbecue pit.

"Thanks," Kep said. "I won't go far. Just down the street a piece." He threw a leg over the bike, slid onto the saddle, and rode away around the garage.

Chester heard the front door of the house close with a loud thump. He dropped his drawing and hurried outside and around the garage.

As Kep rode slowly along the driveway, Oda ran down the front steps, her face distorted and bloodless. Her mouth was open like a person shouting, only no sound was coming out. Her angry eyes flicked across her husband once as she ran. Then she caught the handlebars of the bicycle and shook them with all her strength.

Kep half slid, half fell from the bike, stumbled and fell on the grass at the edge of the driveway, where he lay numbly staring up at the white contorted face with the blazing eyes.

Chester was there then, struggling with his wife. When he succeeded in wrenching the white-knuckled hands loose from the bicycle she gave him a wild look and ran back up the steps into the house.

Kep got to his feet and ran down the walk. Chester stood for a long moment sadly watching him go. Then he took the bicycle back to the shed and went into the house.

As he expected, Oda was in Jimmy's room. She was standing utterly motionless looking out a window. She was seeing only what was far back in her mind, the things she had been keeping alive there for months. He looked around the room at the carefully made bed, the fresh pajamas across the foot of it, the pictures on the walls, the ornaments on the mantle, and he thought, a boy's room and a woman's shrine.

Chester walked three steps toward her, walked the way he always did in her presence, like a man who wants to be assertive but doesn't dare. Apology was reflected in his pale blue eyes, hesitation and anxiety written on his thin face.

"Oda—"

She spun to face him. "Why?" she screamed. "How could you let him ride Jimmy's bicycle? How could you let another boy touch anything that was his?"

He looked into the wild tortured depths of her black eyes. He watched the emotional storm sweeping her, and saw for the thousandth time the terrible weight of her sorrow, and stood helpless as the tide of anguish washed all color from her face. Then abruptly as she

67

stared at him, eyes blazing, her face grew flat and still.

He said softly, "Oda, you shouldn't have done what you did. You've hurt the boy."

Her voice lashed out like an uncoiling whip. "Hurt him. Hurt *him?* What do you think it did to me, seeing him on Jimmy's bicycle? And you permitted him to have it!"

"Oda, listen to me. It's only a bicycle, not any kind of symbol . . ."

"It was Jimmy's." She said it in whimpering desperation. "It was Jimmy's. Everything that belonged to my boy must stay in its place, Chester. It must!"

He watched her cross the room and go out the door, walking with the careful smoothness of high rage.

chapter seven

LINK WYBEL

Kep ran down the drive as fast as he could go until he came to Jackson Street, then he turned south on East Street. He didn't know why he was running except that he always had to run when something bad happened. Right now he had the feeling of being shut up in a box with no air to breathe and the sides of the box squeezing in on him.

At the end of East Street, which was only three blocks long, he came out into an open pasture where a couple of horses and some calves grazed. Here the ground began to slope upward to form the hill that Chester had called Morton's Knob. It was a steep grassy hill with pine trees at the top. Kep ran through a swale where last summer's weed stalks were as high as his

69

head, then up the slope of the hill, which slowed him to a walk.

His lungs were pulling for air by the time he reached the top of the knob, and he fell down on the pine needles. He lay staring up into the cloudless autumn sky while he waited for his chest to stop heaving.

After a few minutes he stood up and looked down on the town and the vast stretch of valley. He sat down with his back against a pine, and knew that this was what he needed, to relax. The breeze out of the north was cool against his face and he liked that. Finally he got up and left the tree to sit in the sunlight so he could feel both the coolness of the breeze and the warmth of the sun.

Later he got to his feet and walked into the woods. He saw that Morton's Knob was the end of a ridge that ran back to join other ridges to the east and south. It felt good to breathe in the spicy smell of the pines.

Two squirrels quieted when they heard Kep coming and began barking and chattering again as soon as he passed. He watched them chase each other up an old dead hickory and disappear into a hole in a high crotch. A crow cawed in the distance.

Kep walked on down the ridge that was an extension of the knob. He could look down the back side of the ridge into a valley of farmlands. Meandering along the

70

floor of the little valley he saw a creek. He went down into the valley and walked along beside the creek listening to it talking to itself, saucy and happy, as if being a creek and running through this valley was the finest thing in the world.

The creek ducked into heavy timber and he followed it around a wide bend to a tall bluff. There he stopped and stood looking at the huge lip of rock and at the wide still pool beneath it. He had the strange feeling, standing alone in the woodland silence, that these trees and rocks and the quiet pool had been waiting here a long time just for him to come to them. He felt more at home among these things of nature than he did with most people.

He walked close to the pool and sat down on a big flat rock at the edge of the water. The underside of the bluff was wet and drippy and covered with patches of moss. He picked up a handful of pebbles and began thumping them one at a time into the still pool.

"There's some mighty fine trout in that pool," a quiet voice said.

Kep looked in the direction of the voice and had to swing his gaze across the timber twice before he saw the man leaning against a swamp hickory not thirty feet from him.

The man chuckled softly. "Did I scare you, boy?"

71

"No, you didn't scare me," Kep said, and wondered why the voice hadn't startled him.

The man pushed away from the tree and came toward him. He was a tall, very lank, wide-shouldered man close to thirty. He had quiet gray eyes, dark skin, and a big nose that had once been broken. On his face was a strange listening silence that let Kep know that here was a man who had lived with the secret and mysterious ways of the outdoors, a man as much at home in the world of nature as in his own home.

The man sat down on the flat rock beside Kep. "Never saw you around here before," he said. "New here?"

"Yeah, I just arrived," Kep told him. "I live with Mr. and Mrs. Maskew. My name is Kep Lanning."

"You live with Chester and Oda?"

"Yes. What's your name?"

"I'm Link Wybel. Maybe you already heard about me."

"No, I ain't."

"You will," Link said dryly. He studied the face of the long-jawed boy, wondering what he was holding inside of him, wondering what he was afraid of. "Yes," he said lazily, "there's some good trout in this pool. The creek's been stocked. So has the lake below town."

"You ever fish here?"

"Plenty of times," Link said. He lay back on the rock and locked his hands over his head. "You ever done much fishing?"

"Some."

"Ever heard hound dogs run in the hills?"

"I never lived where there was hills of any size till I came here. What do the hound dogs chase?"

"Fox. Got some slick ones hereabouts."

"You have?" Kep too lay back and pillowed his head on his hands.

"Yep. A fox has got a lot of tricks he'll use to fool a pack of dogs. You ever hear what a smart fox will do when a pack is pushing him hard?"

"What?"

"He'll double back on his own trail."

"How's he do that?"

"He'll be ahead of the pack a ways, and all at once he'll turn back over his own trail. He'll run back as far as he dares, then cut off at another angle and make his trail into a big V. Well, when the dogs come to the V they'll take the one he ran over twice because the scent is stronger there. Then when they come to where he doubled back they've got no more scent to follow."

"What do they do then?" Kep asked interestedly.

"They snuff around, baying and trying to smell some sense into the riddle. Then finally they back-track, trying to figure out where they went wrong. When they get back to the fork they take the other branch of the V but by that time Mr. Fox has had enough head start that he's long gone from there."

"Well, I'll be dogged!" Kep exclaimed. "Who'd think an animal could figure all that out? I doubt I could have figured it out myself."

"A fox is smart, all right," Link said. "All the woods creatures are smart, if a man understands them well enough to appreciate just how smart they are. Who would you say is the world's best fisherman?"

Kep grinned. "Golly, I wouldn't know. You know?"

"Not a man, I'll tell you that. But I never could decide. Lot of good ones. Ever seen an osprey?"

"Fish hawk? Yeah, I seen 'em in a movie short once."

"Now there's a fisherman, that osprey."

"Ain't he though? He dives for his fish. Sometimes when he gets one an eagle will chase him to get it away from him, did you know that? The osprey gets scared and drops his fish and the eagle catches it in mid-air. You ever see that?"

Link shook his head. "I've heard of it. I'd like to see it. I do know that a fish hawk likes to go after carp because he can see them easy. Carp, you know, are really gold fish—or gold fish are carp, whichever way you want to look at it."

"You mean these little old gold fish people have in bowls are carp?"

"That's right," Link told him. "Gold fish first came from the Orient; they bred them there for size and color. Hundreds of years of cross-breeding. You put one in a big place like a lake and he'll grow big."

"Say, if you saw a dead fish floating around on a pond or a lake with a hole in its side, would you know what killed it?"

Link grinned and said, "You saying a turtle?"

"Yeah, you guessed it!"

They laughed together.

Link said, "There's not an animal that loves fish catching more than rats, did you know that?"

Kep shook his head. "You mean rats will catch fish?"

"They sure will. So will coons and mink."

"Otters too," Kep said excitedly. "I've seen otters down in Florida."

"A family of them lives in the lake south of town. Somebody put a pair in there. There's a pond near my house with a slough running from it to the lake, and the otters come up to the pond sometimes. Hard to get a look at the scapers, though. Bet you didn't know bobcats and foxes would catch fish, did you?"

"I sure didn't," Kep said. "Are there any bobcats around here?"

"Once in a while you'll see one, but they're pretty scarce."

"There's bears down in the Florida Everglades. My pa told me about seeing them there when he was young. He saw them at night, by moonlight, eating leaves from fire-plant. He said they'll stand right up to a bush and pull leaves off and eat them just like a person would."

They lay there on the sun-warmed flat rock in the woodland stillness and talked until the shadows on both sides of the pool had drawn together into one shadow and the setting sun was thrusting red-gold bars of light between the trees.

Link sat up and said, "Well, I guess I'll be moseying for home."

"Gosh, me too!" Kep said. "I'd no idea it was getting so late."

As they walked back along the creek, Kep said, "What's the name of this creek?"

"They call it Badger Creek."

When they came to Morton's Knob, Link pointed down the hill and said, "See that old house down there with all the junk in the yard? That's where I live."

"You live by yourself?"

"Yep."

They talked for a few moments more then Kep said he had better be getting on home, and started down the long slope towards Maskew's house.

Link watched him go and wondered where the boy had come from and why he was living with the Maskews. How in the world could he live with them—with Chester, who never seemed to have any interest in anything but making money, belonging to organizations, sponsoring this and that and being the town's most important citizen? And with Oda, a pitiful creature, a good woman, and a very lively person until she had let grief shrivel her mind. What kind of a home was that for a sensitive lad with a tenseness in him that needed to be soothed?

There was sympathy in Link Wybel, for he remembered what it was like to be a boy, filled with frustration and heartaches. He had known what it was like to be a long way from the only place that had ever been home, and to yearn hollowly for even a little friendliness and companionship and understanding.

A train whistled far up the valley and the sound, sifted by the miles, crept softly around and over the timbered hills.

Link watched Kep come to East Street, where the boy turned and waved. He lifted a hand in reply, then started for home, angling down the slope through the gathering twilight, walking in his usual loping gait, moving as silently as a big cat.

chapter eight

WILL TO TRY

Kep walked fast toward home, not wanting to be any later than he could help. When he went into the house, he found Chester alone in the kitchen washing the dishes.

"Hi," Kep said. "I'm sorry I'm late."

One glance at the boy told Chester that the tenseness created by the bicycle episode was gone now. And he was glad.

"I saved you some supper," he said, tipping his head toward the table.

After Kep had washed up, Chester said, "I was kind of worried about you."

"Oh, I just went roaming around up in the hills. Met a fellow and we talked about birds and animals and
78

stuff. I didn't know it was so late or I'd have come home earlier."

"Who was this fellow you met?"

"Link Wybel is his name. He's sure a wonderful man. Knows all about fishing and stuff, about all kinds of wild animals. Knows just about everything."

Chester focused his attention on the pan he was scouring, so Kep would not see his face. For he knew it would betray his disapproval of the fact that Kep had made friends with Link Wybel. Wybel was the town pariah, the man the better people considered the town's most worthless character.

Chester rinsed the pan and, while drying it, glanced at Kep. He saw that after roaming the woods and meeting Link the boy was feeling more at ease and behaving more naturally than at any time since he had arrived. Seeing this change, Chester no longer felt so disapproving of the boy's friendship with the town bum. He didn't understand how the boy could like such a person as Wybel, but it was obvious that meeting him had changed the lad for the better.

He sat down at the table while Kep ate and apologized for the way his wife had acted about the bicycle.

"Aw, that's all right," Kep told him. "It made me kind of mad for a little bit, but I'm not mad now."

"I'm glad that's your attitude, son," Chester said in

79

relief. "We must remember that she isn't really responsible for some of the things she does. It's just that she doesn't want anything touched that belonged to our son. I think she'll get over it someday. You can have your own things, though. If you want a bicycle I'll buy you one."

"Well, much obliged," Kep said, "but no need your doing that. I'm getting about too old for a bike anyway. I'd not get much use out of it, I reckon. And about your wife, I—I like her all right. Only thing is, I'm just kind of scared to say anything to her."

"I know," Chester nodded. "I think it will all work out in time." Then after a pause he said, "The school principal phoned me a while ago, Kep." He watched the brown eyes drop and the lean face become quiet. "He said you left school today."

"Yes, sir."

"I told him I supposed it was because it was all new to you, and that it would probably take a little time for you to get adjusted. I told him you'd be back to-morrow."

"I won't."

Chester Maskew's thin face was almost habitually marked by restlessness and quick little tatters of apologetic smiles. He was smiling now, apologetically, timidly.

"You mean you don't want to go to school, Kep?"

"I mean I won't go, that's all!"

"Why?"

Kep pushed his plate away and flashed Chester a look of mixed anger and fright. "Because you told her! You told my teacher about me—about—what happened to my pa!"

Chester's timid smile was washing across his face. "Why, yes, Kep. I told her. I thought you might have some difficulty getting settled down to your studies after—after all the trouble you've had. I thought if she knew about it she'd give you a break. She's a nice person, Miss Hammond."

Kep looked at the slight man standing there with his head tilted, thin sloping shoulders bent. He thought, *He's a good man. He wants to be a pa to me, but he just don't know how. He probably didn't know how to be a pa to his own boy.* Kep was sorry for Chester. He liked him. More than anything he longed for a close father and son relationship but he couldn't achieve that by himself, and neither could Chester. So he got up and went to his room without saying anything more.

The next morning Kep had breakfast in the kitchen with Chester. No mention whatever was made of school. After Chester went to his office, Kep returned to his room where he stayed all day except for a quick trip to the kitchen at one o'clock to make himself a cheese sandwich and drink a glass of milk.

During the day he made more than a dozen drawings. All of them went into the wastebasket except two, which he put up on a wall of his room. One was of a man chopping down a tree in the woods and the other was of a high bluff with a pool of still water beneath it and a man in waders whipping a fly rod.

Finally he settled down in an easy chair and read some magazines until he heard Chester come home. Chester exchanged a few words with Oda in the front part of the house, then came on down the hall and rapped on Kep's door.

"Come in," Kep called.

Chester stepped in, smiling, and said, "Well, hi!" He looked about the room. "You've got yourself all fixed up here, haven't you?"

"Yes, sir. Fine," Kep said.

Chester saw the two drawings on the wall and said, "Where did those come from? I never saw them before."

Kep said shyly, "I drew them today. They ain't much good."

Chester stepped over and examined the sketches, then looked at Kep. "What do you mean they're no good? I think they're very good. You should study art."

"Well—I just fool around at drawing."

Chester sat down and said, "I talked to your principal today."

Kep looked away from him.

"After I told him about your trouble at school he suggested that you stay out for, say, the first half of this term. Maybe until after the holidays. He feels you need time to adjust to your new life." He studied Kep's face for a moment, then said, "How do you feel? Do you think that would be the best thing to do?"

"I reckon so," Kep said gratefully. "I—uh—thanks."

"Well, that's the way it'll be then. Now what do you say we have some supper? I'll go wash up."

Kep had supposed there would be just Chester and himself at supper, as before, but when they went to the dinette, Oda was there preparing the evening meal.

Chester cleared his throat and said, "Oda, this is— this is Kep. Kep, this is my wife." He was smiling uncertainly. "I guess it'll seem good to you, Kep, to eat a woman's cooking again, after my cooking. I know it will be to me—"

His voice trailed off into an uncertain chuckle.

Oda gave Kep a somber, unsmiling nod and said, "How do you do, Kep."

Her voice made Kep think of a glass of water with ice in it clinking against the sides.

"How-do, ma'am," he said.

She turned away and went on about her work. Kep didn't know exactly how to behave or what to say to this woman who so far had shown him no friendliness whatever.

When the three of them were seated at the table Chester did all of the talking, striving nervously to lay the foundation for a home life for the three of them. The few times that he put a direct question to his wife she either nodded or shook her head—nothing more.

Kep slyly studied this woman whose son he had come here to replace. She had a narrow face with round cheekbones and dark nervous eyes beneath very dark eyebrows. Her mouth was a straight thin line and her gray-sprinkled dark hair was parted in the middle and swept along the sides of her head, arching over her ears smoothly, then drawn back tightly. It reminded Kep of the folded wings of a bird. She sat stiffly erect on her chair, so erect that she gave the impression of trying hard not to move her slender shoulders.

As he studied her, Kep found himself more and more in sympathy with her. It was plain that her sorrow had caused her to build a kind of steel lining within herself. Once or twice her set expression gave way momentarily to a weary, lost look, but that was the only time her face showed any expression whatever.

84

Because he too had suffered the shock of a great loss, Kep could see her for what she was. She was a woman with all happiness, all pleasures gone from her life, leaving her only the core of her loneliness. He wanted to give her some pleasure again, and Chester too. He wanted to help both of them to have the kind of life they must have had before. He wanted to see them smile, wanted them to be relaxed, the way he had been yesterday by the pool with Link.

When the meal was over, Chester told Oda to go ahead to her room while he and Kep did the dishes. When she was gone, he said to Kep, "Since we've been without a housekeeper I've sort of taken over the dish washing." He smiled. "Now I'm going to have a helper." He tossed Kep the dish towel.

"You sure will," Kep told him. "I used to do all the housework at home after my ma died. I don't mind doing housework at all." Right then he felt as if he wouldn't ever mind doing anything that would please this man who had already done so much for him.

"It may be the wrong thing," Chester said, "depriving her of doing her dishes. She needs work. She keeps busy at housework for hours at a time. You'll see her out doing yard work. She wants to keep busy so she'll have less time to think. I feel guilty, though, letting her

85

do so much. It's a kind of problem trying to figure out what is the best thing for her."

Kep nodded.

"I think she'll gradually change as she gets to know you. I'm sure she'll be different . . . really a different person then."

"If only she'd get to liking me," Kep said earnestly. He was silent a long time then added, "I'm going to try awful hard to make her like me."

chapter nine

TRADE DAY

The next day after lunch, when Chester had
left the house, Kep went to the kitchen and asked Oda
if he could do the dishes for her. She stopped her work
at the sink, stood very still for a moment, then turned
and gave him a slow, dark, haunted look. He stood
there, trying to smile pleasantly, feeling embarrassed.

Finally she said, "No," in a tone so soft he could
barely hear it and turned back to her work.

Kep remembered then what Chester had said about
Oda's keeping busy so she wouldn't have so much time
to think, and he guessed he shouldn't have offered to
help. He didn't know what to do with himself. After he
had stood around awkwardly for a few minutes, he went
to the living room and turned on the television. Then

he wondered whether or not he should have done it. Since Oda didn't come in and tell him to turn it off, he sat on the big couch and watched the program.

An hour later she came to the living room and started dusting the furniture. Again he wanted to ask her if he could help, wanted to tell her how he used to help his ma with the sweeping and dusting, but he didn't. She moved about the room, going at her work almost viciously, her expressionless face haunted by the memory of her tragedy. Kep felt a great surge of pity for her, trying so hard to forget about her son.

It was all he could do to keep from going to her and putting his arm around her shoulders the way he used to do to his ma when she was troubled. He got up and turned off the television and went to his room, where he made more drawings. None of them pleased him so they went into the wastebasket.

The next morning he went to town and stayed until noon just window-shopping around the square and wandering through the stores. He drank a coke at a filling station and that was all he bought for himself. But he went into the dime store and bought Oda a set of pot holders. On impulse he asked the counter girl to wrap them in colored paper and tie the package with ribbon.

He went home to lunch, and when it was over and Chester was gone, he got the package from his room and took it to Oda in the kitchen.

"I—I was in town this morning," he told her shyly, "and I got you a—a kind of a present. It ain't much. I just thought—that I'd get it for you."

She turned her dark eyes on him without saying anything. Finally she put out her hand for the package. When he handed it to her she said, "Thank you," crossed the room, put it on the small table by the kitchen window and went back to her work.

That evening Kep saw that the package was still there, unopened. When he went to bed it still hadn't been touched.

Kep spent his time around the house, most of it in his room, until Saturday afternoon, when he went to town again, intending to go to the matinee at the movie house. As he turned onto Lee Street, he saw a crowd of people gathered on a vacant lot down by the railroad track. There were cars and trucks and wagons parked all around the lot and people milling about as if at a carnival midway.

Kep walked down there and found out that it was a kind of an outdoor market place. The trucks and cars and wagons of farmers were arranged in a large semi-circle and by each vehicle was a display of all sorts of produce. There were crates of eggs, stacks of pumpkins, racks of smoked hams and many other farm items.

He learned that it was Trade Day. He had never heard of such a thing as Trade Day before. Every now and then there would be a momentary buying flurry in one area; then it would die down and another one somewhere else would draw the crowd to it.

There was one man who seemed to be a buyer of dogs. Kep watched him going from one owner to another looking their dogs over. He followed the man along to a wagon where half a dozen grown hounds were on leashes and some pups were running loose.

A straw-haired hill youth about Kep's age was trying to keep the pups shooed away from the old dogs which were up for sale, but every time he would chase them away they'd come right back again. Finally he lost his patience, grabbed a stick and hit one of them a sharp blow across the back legs. It ran screaming in pain and he ran after it. He caught up with it a few feet from where Kep stood and kicked it in the ribs. It disappeared yelping into the crowd.

There was a sudden sickness in Kep, and before he knew what he was doing he took two steps toward the boy. He caught him by the shoulder, spun him around and smashed a fist into his mouth.

The boy's slack look of surprise quickly turned to anger. He backed off a step and landed his fist on the point of Kep's chin. Kep went down, sitting. His head felt like a tea kettle with the steam inside making the lid jiggle up and down. He was instantly on his feet, swinging, but before he was able to land a punch a big hand closed on the upper part of his arm. He turned angrily and looked into the dark grinning face of Link Wybel.

"First round's over," Link drawled. "Didn't you hear the bell?"

"He hit me!" the hill boy screeched. "He hit me and I didn't do nothin' to him first at all."

A crowd of men had gathered and a big-footed man came over and glowered at Kep as he said to Link, "This kid poked my boy in the snoot."

Link, still grinning, said, "Yeah. He should have poked him harder, Mase. Your kid had it coming to him. Maybe you didn't see him kick that hound pup." He still held Kep's arm, and now he swung him around and moved out of the crowd. As they walked away he said to Kep, "I'd like to do the same thing to the old man, but I can't afford to lose a possible customer."

Now Kep noticed for the first time that Link was leading a half-grown hound. The pup was white with splotches of tan all over him like freckles, and he had the longest ears and the saddest eyes Kep had ever seen on a dog.

"Hey, is that your dog?" Kep asked.

"Yeah, he's boot I made on a trade a while ago," Link said.

"Trade? You mean a dog trade?"

"Yep. I'm a kind of middle-man on Hound-dog Day. I buy from the hill boys and re-sell to the buyers."

"Who are the buyers?"

"Couple of guys from Missouri. This thing was left over from my last deal. Can't seem to get rid of him."

Kep knelt by the pup and stroked its ears and patted its bony back. "What's the matter with his foot?" He examined one of the pup's front feet.

"Kind of slew-footed," Link said. "Got it hurt somehow when he was small, most likely."

"Will it ever get straight?"

"No, he'll never be able to do much running. Too bad too. He's good Walker stock."

They walked around the lot for a while and during that time Link made another dog purchase and a re-sale that netted him ten dollars. Then he said he didn't see any more prospects so they might as well go.

"Gosh," Kep said admiringly as they left the lot, "you sure made yourself ten dollars mighty slick there."

"Beats working," Link grinned.

"Ain't you going to try to sell this pup?"

"Maybe next Trade Day. I'll never be able to get more'n a buck or two for him, though."

As they walked down Magnolia Street to Hanover

and turned south, Kep was proudly leading the slew-footed pup and Link was loping along in his cat-like way. The concrete walk of Hanover Street turned into a weathered plank sidewalk which became a foot path outside the town. To the south and east was pasture land that sloped up toward Morton's Knob. To the southwest was more pasture, and beyond it the pond that Kep had seen from the top of Morton's Knob, the pond where Link had said the otter family could sometimes be seen. There was willow growth around the pond and along the slough that ran south toward the timberland where the lake was.

"How long since you saw any otter tracks around that pond?" Kep asked.

"Quite a while. They live at the lake and just come up to the pond occasionally."

"I'd sure like to get me a look at them."

"About daylight would be the best time. Well, here's my mansion," Link told him as they approached the big house Link had pointed out from the knob. "There's the Wybel junk yard."

Kep, looking the place over, thought that was just about what it was. The old two-story house was weathered a scaly brown and the yard fence was sagging and broken. Before the gate was an old pickup truck. The yard was literally stacked with ancient cider presses, millstones, grain cradles, grindstones, ox yokes, and even a high-wheeled hack.

Link led the way through the mounded junk and up onto a gallery that ran the length of the house. On the gallery were piled ancient bureaus, brass beds, spinning wheels, grandfather clocks and countless other dusty and battered relics.

"The remains of yesterday's proud possessions," Link said. "It's junk, but I like to call it antiques."

"Where did you ever get it all?" Kep asked in wonderment.

"Here and there over the state. I repair it and sell it, believe it or not."

"You mean people buy that stuff?"

Link chuckled. "It's hard to believe, isn't it? Yes, I've shipped some pieces as far as California."

Kep tied the bony-hipped pup to a pillar of the gallery and they went around the house to the back yard, which was less cluttered than the front. There was a shed in which were power tools that Link said he used to rebuild his antiques. Connected to the shed was a lean-to where he kept lumber and other materials.

"Come on, let's go inside," he said, and they entered the house through a back door that opened onto a rear gallery.

Kep was astonished at how different the house was on the inside. The huge living room was papered in bright colors, there was a big fireplace against one wall, the furniture was modern and almost as nice as that in the Maskew home. There was a television and a radio, and Kep could see through an open door into a bedroom that was as clean and nice as if a woman lived in the house.

"I think there's some Cokes in the kitchen," Link said. "Come on."

They went to the kitchen, which was furnished with modern equipment. The walls and cabinets were agleam with a recently applied coat of pale blue paint. Link nodded Kep to sit at the kitchen table and he brought Cokes from the refrigerator.

"Gosh!" Kep said, "you got this as toned up as a woman's kitchen."

Link chuckled. "I'm the kind of a cook and house-keeper as needs all the help modern appliances can give."

When they finished their drinks they went out to the front gallery. Kep sat down beside the flop-eared pup and took the leash off him. Link dropped into a battered old rocker and watched Kep stroking the pup and mur-muring to it, talking to it in small friendly broken sounds. Kep lay down, and when he did, the pup was in-

95

stantly all over him, lapping happily at his ears and his face while the boy laughed and rolled and hid his face. Then he got up and ran down the gallery steps as the pup blundered after him.

For the next ten minutes they played hide-and-seek through the maze of relics in the front yard. The pup was the first to quit the game. He came up onto the gallery and flopped down, panting happily. Kep came up the steps and put his head on the dog, using him for a pillow. The pup didn't object.

Kep said, "He's got a right smart of pep, all right."

"He's young," Link pointed out. "In a couple of years he'll be so lazy he'll be leaning against the fence to bark. Unless it's time to go after a fox, that is. He'll come alive then. He won't ever be able to do much though, not with that game foot."

Kep sat up and gave his attention to the pup for a few moments, stroking the long ears, then he said to Link, "Have you always lived here?"

"Born here," Link told him. "I was gone several years."

"Your ma and pa dead, I reckon."

"Long time ago."

"You must like living here, if you came back after being gone several years."

Link stretched his long legs. "I don't rightly know

why I came back. I'm like the woods creatures, I guess. They mostly keep pretty close to one bedground. And I —well, I like to live the way I like to live. No punching a time clock for me. No nine to five job for this old hound dog. To most of the people in this town I'm a no-good, shiftless bum. I reckon they're right. But, like I said, I live the way I like to live."

Kep was silent as he watched the wild colors the setting sun was washing across the western sky. Finally he said, "My pa was a farmer. That is, he was before we moved to town. You ever lived on a farm?"

"Used to work on my uncle's farm, when I was a kid."

"My pa was a real swell fellow." Sitting there, staring at the sunset, Kep did what he thought he would never do again, he told all about how his pa was killed.

But this time it was different, this time he did it because he wanted to, because somehow he wanted Link to know about it. He knew that here was a man who would give him the something he needed, the something that the soul within him had been crying out for ever since that morning his pa was killed. He didn't know what that something was. Then, thinking about it, he did know. It was sympathetic understanding. Not woman pity such as Mrs. Ames had given him, not a desire to help him, like Preacher Barton, but friendly man un-

97

derstanding. He knew he would get that from Link Wybel.

Link, listening to the boy tell of his tragedy, watching
his face, was thinking, *He's got to clear his skies. He's
needing someone to confide in. His confidence is going
to need plenty of building up before he'll be able to handle the lost feeling that's got him.*

When Kep had finished telling his story, he was a-
mazed at how easy it had been to tell it to this man with
his easy manner and fog-gray eyes. Looking up into the
quiet dark face, he suddenly believed he loved Link Wybel as much as he had loved his own pa. Then he was instantly engulfed in feelings of guilt for he should be feeling the same way toward Chester who had already done
so much for him and was planning to adopt him, to give
him a good education.

"How are you getting along with the Maskews?"
Link asked him.

"Oh, all right, I reckon. Only..."

"Only what?"

"Well, I don't know. Chester, he's trying to be a pa.
He's being real good to me. I think he likes me but—
well, we just don't seem to understand each other too
well. I like him. I sure-'nough do. Still I don't seem to
feel about him like I ought to, seeing that he's doing so

much for me. I—I wish I could like him the way I like you."

"Well, now," Link said lazily, "people don't all like each other the same, any more'n all animals like all humans the same. Take dogs now. There are those that like all people, like that hound dog. Then there's others that like only certain people. One-man dogs, you know. Not many of the real wild animals, lions for instance, care much for humans. Yet I knew a fellow once who was the cat man with a little circus. He had an old lioness there that he could do anything with. She was no more dangerous to him than a house cat would be. That old thing really loved him." He was silent a moment then added quietly, "Maybe if you tried real hard you could work up a liking and understanding between you and Chester."

"I've thought about it, and I reckon maybe there would get to be more understanding between us, if I'd try harder."

"And let him see that you're trying," Link told him. "Have you started school yet?"

Kep told all about what happened his first day at the Pine Valley school. "I ain't going back," he said tightly. "I just hate the idea of all the kids looking at me the way the people did back home when they found out I'd shot

99

my pa. They'd soon be just like those people, wanting me to tell them all about it. I told Chester I wouldn't go back. So he talked to the principal and they decided the best thing would be for me to stay out of school for a while."

"I agree with them," Link said thoughtfully. "Now, how do you get along with Oda?"

Kep told all about Oda pushing him off the bicycle. Then he said, "I don't hardly know what to do with myself around there. I never know what I can touch and what I can't. Only I know now that I don't dare touch anything that belonged to her son, that's for sure. I like her, though, and I wish she'd like me. I thought when I came here that she would be like a ma to me. I wish she would be."

The pup stirred and Kep patted him. Then he stood up. "Gosh, I think I'd better be hitting out for home." He started down the gallery steps. "See you."

Link asked, "Aren't you forgetting something?"

Kep stopped. "What?"

"This hound."

"You're giving me a good Walker dog?"

"He'll never be much of a hunter but he'll make you a good buddy."

"He sure will," Kep said happily as he tied the rope around the pup's neck.

100

Link stood up and stretched his long body, reaching his hands high. "Think your folks will let you keep him?"

"Oh, sure. Sure they will. Chester told me I could have anything of my own I wanted."

"What are you going to call him?"

"I don't know. How about Slew, on account of that game foot?"

Link smiled and nodded.

"Well, gosh!" Kep said. "I sure am obliged to you for him."

"You're welcome. A hound is a good companion. Not many breeds have any more affection for humans than the flop-ears."

"Well, I'll see you," Kep said. "And thanks again."

"You can go around back and cut across that way. Be shorter."

"Yeah, I know," Kep said, and was gone.

chapter ten

SLEW-FOOT

Chester, in coveralls and wearing work gloves, was laying brick for the base of his barbecue pit by the light from a back-yard floodlight when Kep came into the yard leading the hound dog.

"Hey, look! I got me a dog!" Kep said.

Chester turned and looked. "Oh?"

"He's a Walker dog," Kep told him proudly, "but he's not much good, though." He squatted and lifted the pup's front quarters. "This foot here got hurt sometime when he was little, so he won't ever be able to run very good."

"Where did you get him?"

"I went to the Trade Day sale in town."

Chester took one glove off, rubbed his hand along

the pup's bony back and fingered the ears that were long enough to be tied together beneath the chin. "You bought him there?"

"No, I didn't buy him. Link gave him to me."

"Who?"

"Link Wybel. He buys and sells hounds down there on Trade Day."

Chester put his glove back on and scraped up a trowel of mortar. "Yes, I know," he said.

There it is again, Kep thought as he watched Chester methodically placing each brick. *We just don't seem to understand each other like we ought to. He doesn't understand how much I want a dog. He doesn't understand how good Link is to me, how we both like the same things ... animals and the hills and the woods and all.*

Then he remembered what Link had said about trying real hard to bring about a better understanding, and letting Chester see that he was trying. He thought maybe he should try to explain how much he wanted a dog.

"I had me a dog," he said, as he fingered a brick, "just before I came here. Well, I didn't have him long. I had to give him up when I came here to live with you. Because I hadn't paid for him yet. I was going to buy him, though, if I'd stayed there."

He said that much and didn't seem able to say anything more, because he was suddenly too discouraged to go on. It was no use. Chester didn't seem to be even listening to him.

Actually, Chester was listening attentively. He knew by Kep's tone of voice how much the dog he'd had to give up had meant to him and how much this bony, slew-footed hound pup meant to him now. It was something that Chester couldn't understand for he had never owned a dog in his entire life. But he honestly did want to feel closer to the boy, to give him the things he wanted and needed. It was certainly plain that he needed this bony pup.

"Well, uh, does it have a name yet?" he asked.

Kep stroked the long ears. "I'm going to call him Slew. Ain't that a crazy name? Maybe I ought to call him Slow, because Link says that foot will slow him down some."

"He looks as if he could stand some fattening up," Chester said.

"Couldn't he though? I'll get him fat, all right. Is it okay if he sleeps in the workshop or the garage?"

"You can put him in the garage."

"I could build him a dog house. I reckon I'll do that tomorrow."

He took the pup to the garage and found some pieces of canvas for his bed. He thought the best thing would probably be to say nothing about the pup to Oda, and let Chester tell her about it. But Chester didn't mention it at supper or at any time before they all went to bed.

WHEN CHESTER came into the kitchen the next morning Oda was already there.

"Did you hear a dog howling all night?" she asked him.

Chester glanced at her and said with quiet timidity, "Yes, I heard it." He knew how she would react when he told her about Kep's pup.

"Why was a dog hanging around here, do you suppose?" she said.

"It's tied out in the garage."

She turned and looked at him quietly, flatly, letting her thoughts lie undisturbed in the thin skeins of haze that clouded her mind. "Who tied a dog in the garage?"

"Kep did. He brought it home."

She stopped all movement. She stood straight and still, looking at him, her black eyes as unmoving as the stars, a kind of puzzled, angry dejection seeming to hold her.

"Every boy wants a dog, Oda," Chester said. "Kep has nothing he can call his own..." Another glance at her face and his words dribbled away to nothing.

"I won't have a dog here! Digging holes in the yard. Fleas! I hate dogs!" Angrily she spun around and was gone.

He watched her leave the room, walking very straight, and wondered how he could tell Kep that he couldn't keep his pup. He decided to put it off until he came home that evening. He got his hat and coat and quietly left the house.

When Chester had driven off, Kep came through the kitchen. He didn't stop, but ran out and down the porch steps as if someone were after him. He dashed into the garage, untied his pup, took him in his arms and ran across the yard, down the slope and south on East Street.

He put the pup down then and led him, hurrying along toward Link's house. He could see a thin rope of smoke standing up from the chimney, which told Link was at home.

When Link heard Kep on the back porch, he opened the door and said cheerily, "I've got flapjacks on the griddle, some melted butter for them and plenty of blackstrap. Come on in."

Kep tied the pup on the porch and went into the kitchen to wash up.

"How many flapjacks can you eat?"

"Oh, three or four, I reckon."

"Is that all? You better make it an even half-dozen."

"How'd you know I hadn't had any breakfast yet?"

Link grinned. "Easy. When the lining of a boy's stomach starts rubbing together it's like two live wires touching. Throws off sparks that come out of his ears, didn't you know that? That's what my hillbilly uncle used to tell me."

When Link joined him at the table, Kep said, "I can't keep Slew." For an instant there was a slight quiver in his tone, then he got control of it. Link waited until he was ready to say more. "I tied him in the garage and he howled all night."

Link nodded.

"I didn't hear him," Kep explained, "else I'd of got up and 'tended to him, so his howling wouldn't fret her."

When Link spoke it was in the gentle tender drawl that was the way his voice always sounded, even when he spoke loudly. "Did they say you couldn't keep him?"

"No, not yet. I heard Oda sharp-speaking about me to Chester in the kitchen this morning. They didn't know I heard it. She said she wouldn't have a dog a-round the place. So I knew Chester would tell me before long that I couldn't keep Slew." He was silent a moment, then said bitterly, "The day she pushed me off the bike Chester told me I could have anything around that I wanted. But I reckon I can't."

"Well," Link said, "I guess it would be bad to have a dog around howling all night. Bad for a sick person, that is, and you've got to remember that Oda is a sick woman."

"Yeah, I know it. I don't want to do anything to make things worse for her. The main reason I came here was to try to help her, and I don't want to do anything that might make her not like me."

"Well now, maybe you haven't been able to help her much yet," Link admitted, "but it's way too soon to say that you won't ever be able to. It takes anybody a time to get adjusted to a change. A woman in the state she's in—why, it'll probably take a good deal longer than it would a normal person."

"You think she might get to like me after a while?" Kep asked eagerly.

"I think it's likely she will, given time. Anyhow I'm glad you're not going to keep the pup over there. I got to thinking about it last night."

"Why?"

"Well, now you figure, that pup's never going to have much of a life. A hound is born to run and trail, and with that foot of his, he'll never be able to get around very good. So it would seem to me that the least we can do is see that he's got his freedom, to go limping around all he wants to."

Kep nodded.

"If you kept him over there you'd probably have to keep him tied up. Oda would never stand his running loose, that's for sure. Then what kind of a life would he have? Best thing would be to leave him here with me. He can be your dog just the same. Here he can do just as he pleases, in and out of the house, anything he wants to do. If you want to take him up in the hills, come and get him any time. How about that?"

Kep was touched, but tried hard to smile as he said, "That's about the best thing that's happened to me, seems like, for a good spell."

After they had washed the dishes, Kep helped Link in his workshop until mid-afternoon, then he went on home to do anything he could to help Oda. The only thing he could find to do was straighten up some things in the garage for Chester.

He was still there when Chester came home, so he told him right away about the arrangement to leave the pup with Link.

"He'll stay there all the time," he explained, "but he'll still be my dog just the same. I can go over there and play with him any time I want, and I can take him to the woods. Do anything I want to with him. You think that's all right?"

He was eagerly watching Chester's face.

"Sure it's all right," Chester said, smiling his thin smile.

He was thinking, *At last I can say "yes" to Kep about something that he wants. He's a boy of nature and needs to have a dog to run with him in the woods. Besides, if he has other interests he won't be around the house so much. That will be best until Oda has time to get to know him and adjust to his being here.*

Kep said, "Gosh, I'm so glad about having my dog! Thanks a lot! How about if I help Link with his work around his shop there? I helped him today. I could do a lot for him. He's been mighty good to me, giving me the pup. Would that be okay?"

Chester's first thought was of Link Wybel's reputation and his way of life. But one glance at Kep's eager young face, and he said that was all right, too.

EVERY DAY when there was nothing at home to be done, Kep went to Link's house and worked with him in his workshop. Link gave him such jobs as building crates and packing pieces for shipping. He loved the work, the feeling of accomplishment, the comradeship with Link.

Saturday afternoon they were packing two pieces that were going to be shipped to Texas. They were nearly finished when they heard Slew let out an excited yip and turned to see a rabbit streak past the yard. A moment later the pup came out of the weeds, looked all a-round, and began nosing for the trail. He picked it up almost instantly and went gamboling away, throwing his injured foot awkwardly as he ran.

Watching him, Kep sighed. "He sure ain't going to be much of a runner, with that game foot."

"He'll have fun," Link told him.

"I'll bet he could pick up the trail of the otter family down at the lake," Kep said excitedly. "How many you think there are in the family?"

"Ma and Pa and Junior, from the looks of the tracks I've seen."

"I'm going to get up early every morning and go down to the pond and watch for them."

"You might spend all winter and not see them," Link warned. "While you're scouting the pond they might be away down around the lake somewhere."

"I'll go down there sometimes too. I'm going every day for a while and see if I can get me a look at them."

chapter eleven

AT THE LAKE

Before going to sleep that night Kep set the
alarm clock in his mind to wake him up at four the next
morning, which it did. After the first time he had no
trouble waking at that time every morning. He would
get up, dress and go quietly to the kitchen where he
would eat a slice of bread with jam and drink a glass
of milk. Then he would go to Link's house, get Slew
from the lean-to shed, and strike out for the pond. By
the time daylight came he would be hidden somewhere
in the willows at the edge of the pond, his jacket buttoned up to his chin, his eyes scanning the surface of
the gray-brown water. Slew would spend his time in the
brush trying to pick up a trail. When the sun was well
up, Kep would call him and they would go to Link's

house for breakfast. Kep went to the pond before day-light every morning for a week but not once did he get a glimpse of the otters. So he decided to try down at the lake.

The next morning he got up a half-hour earlier, hur-ried to Link's, got Slew, and headed for the lake. The first dawn light was spreading up the eastern sky when he arrived at the lake, which was in a woodland section surrounded by thickly growing timber. He made his way among the trees along shore until he came to a place where a spit of willow-grown land thrust several yards out into the lake. He pushed his way through the wil-lows to the tip of the out-thrust and settled himself in a spot where he was well concealed and had an unob-structed view of the lake surface. When the day broad-ened a little, he could see every foot of the lake clearly. Slew was off somewhere in search of a scent, and Kep sat quietly in his blind, watching the day come alive out on the water.

Then suddenly it happened! A whiskered muzzle broke the glassy surface of the lake and there was the head of a male otter. Kep got so excited he almost laughed out loud.

The otter thrust himself high out of the water and be-gan rolling and diving. His movements were so smooth they barely disturbed the surface of the water. Then suddenly a female otter and a young one surfaced at the same time. The pup was the cutest thing Kep had ever seen. It kept trying to climb up onto it's mother's back and she would push it off and duck it.

After a few minutes of play the otters, led by the male, swam ashore, crawled out and started searching in the mud for a crawfish breakfast. The pup ran on ahead of its parents, who moved more slowly, doing a more thorough job of hunting.

All at once Kep noticed a disturbance in the bank growth near the spot where the pup was scooting along. The boy got on his knees for a better look and saw Slew plunge out of the brush and grab for the otter pup. At the same instant the mother hit the water and the male went flopping across the mud toward Slew, who was yelping his excitement and trying again and again to grab his prey. The little otter was able to dodge Slew only because of the dog's game foot, but when they got into shallow water Slew grabbed the pup in his jaws and tossed it into the air. Kep was on his feet yelling at Slew but the hound didn't hear him.

Both the parent otters were converging on Slew and the pup, the mother from the water and the male up the muddy bank. The male got there first. He plunged into shallow water, disappeared for a moment and came up

114

with his jaws clamped onto Slew's throat. The otter pup had scrambled for deeper water, where its mother got behind it and drove it straight out into the lake.

Slew fought desperately to free himself from the male otter but couldn't. Besides his immaturity he had the disadvantage of having only three good feet. With deadly coolness the otter began dragging the hound into deeper water.

Kep started running and screaming, hoping that his shouts would scare the otter off. He grabbed a stick and ran as hard as he could go along shore, clawing his way through reeds and brush growth. Before he could get to them, the otter had dragged Slew out into deep water, and then both disappeared. Kep told himself they would come up again. They just had to come up! He said it aloud, said it wildly, frantically. "They've got to come up."

But they didn't come up. He stood there a long time, and when he finally saw the male otter break the surface far out, he dropped his stick and waded out onto dry land. He started for home, his fists clenched in his pockets, his eyes filled with tears, a hot choking hatred for the otter spreading through him like a disease.

As he slogged along, his mind was screaming, *Why? Why? Why? Why? Why does something always have to happen to everything I love? Why can't I have just one thing that I love without something taking it away from me?*

He trudged along, bent stiffly forward, arms heavy at his sides, his sadness an ache all through his body. Tears ran down his cheeks and dribbled off the point of his long chin. When Kep reached the gallery, Link was in the kitchen, cooking breakfast. He called, "Come in, boy!" Link glanced at his face, then didn't look at him again. "Pull up," he said cheerily. "You look as if you've been up quite a while. Bet you're as empty as a drum."

Kep went to the bathroom and washed his face and hands. Then he came back to the kitchen and sat down at the table without saying anything. Link poured some coffee and sat down too. When their eyes met Kep managed to find a smile somewhere that felt as if it hadn't been used in years.

As they began to eat, Link watched him fighting to handle his troubles manfully. Link knew how it was at such a time. Many times as a boy he too had fought like that for courage, and it was always like trying to harden molasses over a fire.

Finally Kep said, "Link."

By his tone Link knew that he couldn't make it just yet. "I didn't hear you come past this morning," he said, giving Kep time. "You must have been mighty quiet."

"Link."

"Here, how about a couple of eggs?"

"Link."

Link looked full at him then. "All right, son, tell it."

"I—I saw the otters."

Link waited. Now he knew what had happened because he had noticed that the hound pup hadn't come back with Kep.

Kep gritted his teeth, then blurted out, "The—old one he—got Slew. He—dragged Slew under the water and he didn't come up any more." He looked at his plate in silence, then his fist lifted and came down on the table so hard the crockery jumped. "I'll kill him!" he said grimly. "That's what I'll do! I'll hunt him down... I'll hunt that otter till I find him and I'll kill him!"

Link glanced at the taut young face and knew that Kep really meant it. This was no time to beat down his spirit and frustrate him by trying to talk him out of it. After all that had happened to him he'd have to win a battle pretty soon or it wouldn't be long until he'd never fight another one.

"Well, I wouldn't blame you," he encouraged in his slow drawl. "I'd do the same thing. I got a .22 rifle in my bedroom. You can take it and go out in the morning and get that scaper."

As Kep flashed him a look, Link saw the fear, hot and torturous, begin to seep up from the cellars of the young mind. He watched it run down the lank face and settle around the white, stiff mouth. At first he didn't know why, but then he remembered. It was his mention of a gun. The boy was deathly afraid of guns because of what had happened to his father. Here was real tragedy: a boy who would go all through his life without the courage even to touch a gun. Something must be done for him, but not right now.

When they had finished eating, Kep offered to clean up the dishes.

"Well, all right," Link said. "I'll go out and get to work. You going to help me today?"

"Yeah, sure."

"Good! I've got to put a back in that oak highboy and it'll be ready for sanding."

At noon they had lunch. Then Link said, "You can clean up around the shop, if you want to. I've got to go to town. Won't be gone long."

"All right," Kep said.

Link was back in an hour. Kep was stacking some crate lumber against the side of the lean-to when he looked up and saw Link coming around the corner of the house. He had a cardboard box under his arm.

"Come in the house, Kep," he called. "I want to show

you something." They went into the kitchen together and he put his box on the kitchen table and said, "Open it."

Kep looked at him, puzzled. "Me?"

"Yeah."

"But why?"

"Why? Don't you ever figure to get paid for the work you do? You've been helping me around here for quite a while now."

"But it ain't work. I like to help."

"Open it."

Kep broke the paper tape and lifted the lid of the box. His body stiffened. He closed his eyes. His hands began to shake.

"Put it together," Link said.

Kep opened his eyes and caught his lower lip between his teeth. Then he stared into the box and said, "I can't! I can't! Don't ask me why, I don't know why! I just can't!"

When Link spoke, his voice was a lean dry sound and his wide lips chopped together, grinding out the words. "Put it together, Kep."

Kep looked up, startled. He hadn't heard the big man speak in that tone before.

His stricken gaze clung to the dark somber face for a long moment, then his shaking hands reached for the

119

gun. After three attempts he managed to fit the barrel to the stock and tighten the setscrew.

"Here," Link handed him a box of cartridges. "We're going into the hills and see if we can find us a couple of red squirrels."

He got his own rifle and they went out toward Morton's Knob. He did all the talking as they walked along. Once he put a hand on Kep's shoulder as if to tell him that this was something that had to be done and that he shouldn't be afraid.

Kep had difficulty keeping up with Link's long strides because he felt numb inside and out. Even though he was gripping his rifle tightly in his right hand, he was barely able to feel it. They had been walking the deep timber for a half-hour, moving cautiously and quietly down the back slope of the first ridge, when Link lifted a hand and they stopped.

"There, son. On top of that high limb on the left of the tall gum tree," he whispered. "See his tail moving in the breeze? Bring him down." He was pointing.

Kep looked at him, trying to smile. He felt the stiffness of it in his cheeks and up in his forehead. His mind felt clumsy, his throat felt filled with a bitter powder. He fumbled with the rifle but his fingers wouldn't behave. Link, without saying anything, gently took the gun from

120

him, loaded it, threw a cartridge into the firing chamber and handed it back.

"The safety is still on," he said, and watched Kep try frantically to push the safety off. Link knew the pain, the sickness he was causing the boy, but none of the sympathy he felt showed on his dark face. When at last Kep had the rifle ready to fire, he said to him, "Now pull down slow on him, son."

Kep raised the gun uncertainly, trying with everything in him to keep his hands steady. He felt a cold trickle of sweat run down across his ribs. He took aim and pulled the trigger. The squirrel remained on the limb undisturbed. He lowered the gun, the blood pounding so hard in his head that it made him want to turn and run.

He looked up pitifully at Link and numbly pushed the gun at him. "I can't! I just don't want to!"

"Try again, boy," Link said quietly. "We've come out here to put fear in its place. And we'll get the job done. Now try again." Kep raised the rifle and fired again. Nothing. "Again," Link said softly. Kep triggered again and the squirrel's tail twitched. "A shade too low," Link said almost in a whisper. "Come up just a hair. Don't jerk the trigger. Get your aim; then squeeze like you were squeezing a rubber ball."

Kep aimed and squeezed. The squirrel, high on the limb, twitched, swung to the under side of the limb, finally let go and fell to the ground. Link went over and picked it up.

When he came back he stood looking at Kep, and saw the tenseness draining from his face and the fear from his eyes.

"Put your safety on and stand your gun against that tree," Link commanded.

When Kep had followed his orders, Link walked over, and knocked the gun to the ground with his toe. "Pick it up, check the safety and stand it up again." Kep did and Link pushed it over again. "Pick it up and check the safety." Again Kep obeyed. "Guns don't go off accidentally if they're handled properly," Link said evenly. "Let that fact sink into your mind so you'll never forget it, son." After a pause he said, "You feeling better now?"

Kep could feel his mind thawing out, becoming soft and pliable, the way frozen mud will when a hot sun begins to shine on it. He could grin now without feeling the stiffness.

"I—yes," he said. "Yes, I am."

"Good. Pick up your gun. We're going to go find a couple more squirrels. You .come to my house in the morning and we'll have them for breakfast with gravy and biscuits." As they walked on, he studied Kep's face, and suddenly he began to grin. "Want me to tell you who you reminded me of?"

"When?"

"When you were so scared of a gun."

"Who did I remind you of?"

"A guy in my outfit in the army. High tension. Got the shakes over nothing at all. He was scared at target practice, at live ammunition drill, on maneuvers. Everything made him so scared and sick he'd have to go to the hospital and take shots to settle him down. The doctors at the hospital knew, of course, that there was nothing physically wrong with him, and they got tired of his showing up there every few days and taking up their time. So they figured out a way to cure him."

"What did they do? How did they cure him?"

"Something like the way I did you. Scared him worse than he had ever been scared before. They got a veterinarian's hypodermic needle, about a foot and a half long, and when the guy saw them coming at him with it he squealed like a stuck pig. Believe me, when he got out of there that time he never showed up again."

They laughed together, then went on with their hunting. When they got back to Link's house three hours later, they had five squirrels, and Kep had shot every one of them.

"This is a great rifle," he told Link happily as they cleaned their guns on the back porch. "I sure do appreciate you getting it for me."

"You earned it. You're handling it okay now, too."

When he had cleaned his rifle, Kep stood up and said, "Well, it's getting late so I'll have to go. I think I'd better leave my rifle here. I don't think Oda would want me to have a gun around the house."

"Sure," Link said. "Here, give it to me and I'll put it away."

Kep started to hand it to him but decided not to. "You know, I think I'll put it in the workshop so I can get it early every morning without waking you up. I'm going down to the lake every morning at daylight until I get me that otter."

"Okay, you do that," Link said, not missing the tightness of Kep's lips and the quivering of his jaw muscles.

"I'll see you," Kep said, and went to the shop to put his rifle away before he headed for home.

Watching him go, Link grinned to himself and thought, *It'll be good for him to be able to feel that he didn't let Slew down. But if the game warden catches him shooting the otter—well, the law can't do anything to him because he's underage. They sure can do something to me though, for furnishing him the gun and encouraging him to do it.*

124

chapter twelve

THE OTTER FAMILY

Kep followed the same routine as he had when he was making trips to the pond to watch for the otters. He would get up early, go quietly to the kitchen for a slice of bread with jelly and a glass of milk, before taking off for the lake.

When he came back, he would do anything he could see to do that would help Oda with her housework. He would take out garbage and old newspapers, sweep the porches and walks and rake and burn the leaves. He would also help Chester whenever anything needed doing around the garage or the workshop, never waiting for Chester to ask him to do it.

With Link's help, Kep had lost his uncertainty and his fear. It was like being out of prison to be free of

125

those bad things. Now he wanted to help Oda free herself from her mental prison too. He felt if he could get
her to like him it would help, but nothing he did seemed
to do any good. She never smiled at him, never spoke
to him in kindness. In fact, she never spoke to him at
all unless it was absolutely necessary.

Now that he himself had found freedom from fear
and confusion, Kep realized more sharply the troubles
that Chester had had to face up to the past year. First
his son's death, then his wife's turning against him, and
finally Oda's dislike of Kep himself, whom Chester had
brought to take their son's place. Kep was very sorry
for Chester, and spent almost every evening with him,
wanting with all his heart to give this man the companionship he seemed to need.

But that was at night. Every morning Kep would
hurry to Link's house for his rifle and be at the lake
when day broke. At first he would go to the spot where
Slew had drowned, sitting out on the bushy point as he
had done that morning, believing that eventually he
would get a shot at the old male.

Then he would circle the lake, and about noon head
back to Link's house and have lunch with him. In the
afternoons he would work with Link in the shop or go
back home, if there was anything that needed doing
there.

Each day, in his search for the otters, his knowledge of woodcraft grew. He began to see things in the woods that a month before would never have caught his attention. He learned the causes of dozens of small sounds that the inexperienced would never even hear. He learned how the woods creatures hunted their prey, and how the lesser ones protected themselves. He saw quail crouch and blend with the grass and weeds about them when a hawk passed over. He saw a fox standing in a clump of grass weaving back and forth with the wind-blown movement of the grass as it eyed him. He watched a mother fox teaching her young to catch mice.

It was on a Wednesday morning that he found the place where the otter family had left the lake to head across country. Kep crossed over the ridge to the creek and picked up their tracks near the pool under the bluff, where they had stayed a while before starting upstream.

All day long he doggedly followed their faint trail. The sun was low in the west when at last he came upon fresh pad marks in the clay at the edge of the water where the creek made a sharp bend. The boy's heart began thudding wildly against his ribs when he realized how close he was to them.

He followed the spoor a few yards farther and found what he had expected; the otters had left the creek. Furthermore he knew where they were heading. They would go through the patch of pasture swamp ahead, then swing around through the sapling thicket at the foot of the slope and back to the lake. He was so familiar with their habits that he knew for certain where they would cut through the stand of saplings. There was a cleared strip through it that had once been a logging road, and there was heavy brush growth along both sides of it. The otters would follow the worn tracks where the going would be easiest for their short legs. By cutting across, up the ridge and back down, Kep could be there waiting for them when they showed up. He was grinning as he started up the slope to head them off.

When he came to the road he stopped and knelt by a tall rotting stump. It wasn't long until he heard a soft rasping, snarling sound and the rattle of brush.

He raised his head an inch and saw the otter family there on the road, all bunched together. The old dog otter, his back clawed and bleeding, was snarling at his family, trying to move them along the road faster than they could go.

Suddenly he turned to face in the opposite direction as a bobcat came slinking out of the roadside brush, crawling on its belly, hacking and spitting, teeth bared, ears flat. The old otter flopped toward the cat in a quick charge and it backed away from him. At that instant another cat shot out of the brush as if someone had kicked it out into the road. It made a pass at the otter pup who was cowering beside its mother, but the old dog whirled and drove the second cat off. The otter was floppy and unsuited to the land. Thus he was at a disadvantage with the nimble, lightning-fast cats, but he was a fighter, and he was all over the road. He whirled and leaped and flopped about to meet each challenge.

One of the cats tried again for the pup but the mother protected it, then the old dog clashed with the cat, took a claw-raking, and gave out some punishment himself, before he whirled in time to clamp his teeth into the other one.

Then suddenly all activity stopped. The otters crouched together in the middle of the road. The bobcats lay flat, glaring at their quarry, ears pinned back and yellow eyes blazing.

Kep had been watching the battle breathlessly but now, with the action temporarily stopped, he suddenly admired the otter family so much that he wanted to yell at them not to give up. It gave him a chill of pleasure to see how the old dog was crouched and ready to defend his family to the last. Without thinking, Kep threw his rifle to his shoulder, aimed quickly at the two cats crouched in the twilight, and triggered. The bullet splashed dirt between them and they both sailed into the air as if they'd been sitting on a cocked spring. Then they disappeared noiselessly into the brush.

The dog otter watched the spot where they vanished for a few seconds, then shook himself, swung around and drove his family down the road ahead of him into the heavy twilight. When the otters were out of sight, Kep shouldered his rifle and walked out of the thicket.

As he went toward town, he thought back over the many days he had come to the woods with his rifle in search of the otters, and a surprising fact became clear in his mind. He had thought all along that he wanted to kill the otters because they had killed his dog. Now he knew that he hadn't really wanted to kill them at all. He had actually been coming to the woods to think about himself and Link and the Maskews, especially Oda. He would probably have caught up with the otters much sooner if he had been thinking only of them, but he hadn't. Now that the otter hunt was over, he realized that his mind had gone right back to Oda again.

The urge in him to help her get over the problem that was deadening her mind was particularly strong now. It had been in his thoughts ever since Link had helped him clear his own mind, but it was even stronger now. He just couldn't think of any way that he could help her, that was the trouble. All he could do, he supposed, was hope that she would finally get to like him. If she ever did, he felt sure that they could have a relationship that would someday make her forget her awful sorrow.

He stopped to have supper with Link, and when they were seated at the table Link told him "It's my guess that you finally caught up with the otters. This is the first time you've brought your rifle into the house instead of putting it in the shop."

"Yeah, I caught up with them. There was a couple of bobcats after them. And you ought to have seen that old dog otter tie into those cats! Boy, what a battle! I never saw such a thing before."

"I'd like to have seen it," Link said.

"It was really a fight. The cats were trying to get to the pup and the old dog fought them off. I took me a shot at the cats but missed."

"Oh, you shot at the cats, eh? I thought you'd have shot the dog otter."

"No," Kep said sheepishly. "It's funny, but I couldn't shoot him. He killed Slew all right, and he'd of killed those cats too, if he could have. But both times he was only protecting his family. I just got that figured out as I watched him fighting the cats."

Link was smiling as he passed the plate of biscuits to Kep. "You're coming along, son," he said in his slow way. "You've now learned something that many people never learn, that hatred isn't the answer to anything."

chapter thirteen

RIDGE TOPPING

One evening Kep and Chester were watching television when Oda, having finished her work in the kitchen, joined them in the living room. She picked up a book and sat down and read for a few minutes. Then she closed the book abruptly and put it down.

"Kep," she said sharply, "I'd like to talk to you."

"Yes, ma'am," Kep said, startled.

Chester turned the volume down on the television set, then both he and Kep looked inquiringly at Oda, who was sitting very straight, her face expressionless, her lips a thin line. The light above the mantle cut down across her angular profile.

"Kep," she said after a moment, "I haven't given you any orders at all since you've been here. I've left that to Chester, since he was the one who arranged for you to come here. But something has come up that I cannot allow."

Kep stammered, "Why—I—I didn't know I'd done anything I shouldn't have, Mrs. Maskew."

She looked at Chester. "Why didn't you tell him?"

"I don't know what you're talking about, Oda," Chester told her in his mild, grainy voice.

"About Link Wybel." She looked coolly at Kep. "You've been hanging around that man's house. You were even in town with him, weren't you?"

A hot sullen rebellion began to rise in Kep. "Yes, ma'am," he answered quietly. "I've been to his house and I was with him in town on Trade Day."

"Well, we can't have you going there any more."

Kep tried to smile but knew it must look as if he were about to cry. "Why not, Mrs. Maskew? Link's been awful good to me."

"He's not a fit person for you to associate with. He's —he's just worthless. He's an outcast in this town and has been for years. No self-respecting person ever associates with him."

Kep caught his lower lip between his teeth and held it for a moment. Then he repeated stubbornly, "But he's been good to me."

"Perhaps." A severe harshness crept into her voice.

"But he's not good for you. You must not go to his house again or go anywhere with him."

Kep rose to his feet and stood a moment with his hands hanging loosely at his sides, his lips pressed in a straight line. Then he started toward the hall.

Oda called to him, "You understand what I've been saying, don't you?"

He stopped and turned. "Yes, ma'am."

"Then you'll stay away from that man from now on?"

"No, ma'am."

The two words seemed to clatter around the room like a gunshot. Kep could see her shoulders twitch with the shock of them. He was sorry he'd had to say them.

He spoke to her quietly, spoke as an adult, not as a fifteen-year-old boy. "I'm sorry I can't mind you, Mrs. Maskew, but I can't. Ever since I came here I've tried to do things to please you, but I can't do this because Link is my friend. He—he—. He's my friend." He turned and went down the hall.

When he was gone, Oda spoke sharply to Chester. "Are you going to see that he doesn't disgrace us before the whole town?"

Chester finally answered her, his voice dry and lifeless in the big room. "I'm not going to tell the boy who he can and cannot associate with, so long as he behaves himself."

134

"But for him to be running around with that—that—"

"Look, Oda. I brought the boy here because he needed help. He's had a terrible shock. I thought the two of you would be good for each other. Not once since he's been here have you shown him the least bit of affection."

She lifted her face and looked at him in hazy, helpless consternation. "I could never put him or any other boy in Jimmy's place!"

"You could at least treat him kindly. I brought him here to raise as a son and he has to live in the poorest room in the house. He's afraid to touch anything around the place for fear he'll be doing the wrong thing. He wanted love and companionship from us and doesn't get them. Now that he has found warm friendship you're objecting to it."

"But it's—it's—Link Wybel!"

"So it's Link Wybel. I know he's never been a credit to the town, but boys like him. Whatever else he is he's a companion to them. Boys—all boys like a man who goes into the woods for hunting and fishing and such. It's what boys need. It's what Kep needs."

"Then why," she asked spitefully, "don't you go hunting and fishing with him instead of letting him disgrace us before the whole town?"

Chester blew through his lips in a gesture of patience and shook his head. "No, I wouldn't do that. I don't think the boy is especially fond of either of us now, but I'm sure that he respects us. I won't deprive him of that respect by trying now to horn in and win his favor from someone who gave him companionship when we didn't. No, if he has any respect for us left, I refuse to destroy it." He studied her for a moment. Then he brought a hassock from the other side of the room, sat down before her, looked up into her face and said tenderly, "Oda, look at me, dear."

She gave him a hazy half-smile.

"Oda, let's change all this. Let's separate all the important pieces and throw away the bad ones. We can put the good ones back together and have a whole life again, a good life together like we used to have. What do you say?"

Her thin smile wilted and limped off her face. She looked straight at him, and for some reason he couldn't have explained he had to steel himself against her look, had to force himself to hold her gaze.

"It's wrong, Oda. It's cowardly to die in your heart before death actually comes."

"I didn't want to, Chester," she whimpered. "It—it just happened. I didn't want to."

136

"You could help yourself by not doing some of the things you do. Think now. Every week you launder Jimmy's clothes, his shirts, his jeans, everything. Then you put them away in his room and the next week you wash and iron them all over again. Let's change all that, Oda. Let's get rid of everything in that room, clear everything out, re-decorate the room, re-furnish it. If you don't want to put Kep in there then rent it out to a schoolteacher or someone. Let's do something to make a change, Oda. You can't go on like this."

She sat a long time staring into the fireplace, then she looked up at him as if what he'd said had just then reached her mind. As she thought about it, heartbroken righteousness blazed in her eyes. He could see it spread through her like a transfusion. Then it went out of her eyes and for a moment her shoulders sagged. Finally she straightened them, stood up and walked down the hall to her own room. He listened to the door close behind her.

THREE DAYS LATER Link and Kep planned, while working in Link's shop, to make a trip into the hills that night to hear the hounds on a fox chase.

"I was talking to some of the hill boys in town today,"

Link said, "and they're fixing to go ridge-topping tonight."

"That's fox chasing?"

"Yep. You go up on a ridge and build a fire and have yourself a time listening to the chase. Want to come?"

"You bet. I'll be over right after supper," Kep told him.

He was back at seven-thirty, and they struck out together toward the ridges. They were soon in the woods and grading up-slope. The night was curtained in black plush, and smelled of leaf mold, wintering tree bark, and dew that was about to become frost. Just as Kep and Link topped the first ridge, the full moon climbed over the eastern hills, casting its yellow light through the timber.

"Wind's down good tonight," Link commented. He stopped and felt the grass. "This is a night for fox, all right."

"I want to hear them on trail," Kep said excitedly. "I've never been on a fox chase. I always supposed you took guns with you."

"No," Link said, "we don't kill the fox. We like a fox to stay around in our hills, so we can chase him year after year. You see, the sport of this kind of a chase is just to sit and listen to the hounds talk. When you know the dogs and are used to hearing them on trail,

138

they'll let you know just how things are going on the chase every minute, providing you understand their kind of talk."

"Well, what do you know!" Kep exclaimed. "Can you understand their talk?"

"Pretty well. All the dogs around these hills I've heard many times."

They came onto the crest of a high ridge where clouds of stars huddled low, their light now paled by that of the moon.

"Anywhere along here is a good place to settle," Link said. "Let's get us a fire going."

"I can see a fire way down the ridge," Kep told him.

"Yeah, some of the boys will be casting out pretty soon."

They gathered leaves and wood to get their fire going and hunkered close to it for warmth. They hadn't been waiting more than ten minutes when a hound sounded far down the slope of the ridge.

Listening, Kep said, "Is that all the sound they make?"

"No, they're not started yet," Link told him. "You won't hear much out of them till they get a good scent." He had no more than said it when a great deep gonging bellow rolled up from the hollow below. "There!" That's Dave Peters' old Drum, one of the finest dogs anywhere." At that moment another voice sounded. "Hear that? That's Sid Morgan's Chocker."

Suddenly a dozen other voices joined the pack, and the trail song rolled up the ridge, plaintive and rich and blending in golden harmony. Link named the dogs for Kep. He knew each one by its voice.

All of a sudden another throat opened up, a voice that sang out above all the others. Link jumped to his feet and said to Kep, "Hark to that!" They listened to the new clean high tones that rode up the hollows like the ring of a bugle on a cold dawn. Link said tensely, "Now you're listening to one of the sweetest little ladies that ever laid down a muzzle. That's Harley Bates' Silver Girl. Man, what a dog! Listen to her single out! Listen to her tell those other dogs to hold on, that she's coming. Boy, how they're going to need her before the chase is over."

Kep had caught the spirit of the hunt. Goose flesh was creeping along his spine. He stood shifting from one foot to the other and snapping his fingers nervously.

"Now she's got it!" Link said excitedly. "Silver Girl's there with the others now. She's grabbed the trail! Took it right away from them, snatched it right out from under old Drum's big nose!"

Kep laughed with excitement, laughed almost hysterically. "She must be some dog, all right."

140

Link spoke almost reverently. "In her, you're hearing hound music that's come down from all the yesterdays of early America, boy. Her ancestors ran in the years of Daniel Boone. Her kind lived back there on the Wilderness Trail, lived in the days of the shuck ticks and puncheon floors and the Kentucky long rifles."

The chorus began to fade, so Kep and Link again sat down by their fire. They listened to the waning sound that was like wild geese flying high in the night. They sat in the silence with only tiny night sounds around them. The pack drew away southward and the chorus stretched out thin and faint, a silvery thread of sound that shimmered far off in the moon-misty distance for a few moments, then was gone.

Kep let out a long breath and said, "Golly, but that was sure something! Are they gone for good now?"

"No, they'll be back. Old fox he'll ankle south for a ways, then circle back, working out tricks that he hopes will fool the dogs."

"What if he can't fool them?" Kep asked.

"Then he'll hole up in a den somewhere where the dogs can't get to him, and the chase is over."

Three times more the hounds brought the fox within hearing distance, and the third time the tone of the hunt suddenly changed.

Link got to his feet and said, "Well, that's it. Mister

141

Fox has holed up." A horn sounded, then a second one, far down the ridge. "The boys are calling them in. That's all for tonight."

They put their fire out and headed back down the ridge toward home, walking briskly through the chilly night. In Kep's mind he was still hearing that distant musical *owk! owk! owk!* of the pack. "Can I come out with you again?" he asked Link.

"Sure, any time. I come out at least once a week through the fall and most of the winter. I'm always glad to have company."

"Well, you'll sure have it," Kep said happily.

chapter fourteen

THE PATCH

On a Saturday just before the holidays Chester told Kep he could help burn off a lot that he owned, a couple of blocks down from the house, if he cared to.

"Sure, I'd like to," Kep told him.

Chester went in the house and changed to work clothes, and when he came out Kep was waiting for him. "Shall I get a rake or hoe or anything," he asked.

"No," Chester said, "we'll just set the fire and watch that it doesn't get out of hand. There's no wind so that won't be a problem."

They walked down to the vacant lot and went to work. At one end of the lot the weeds were tall and thick. They burned these off first. As the fire worked into the short grass it didn't require much attention.

There was a low wall of an old foundation in the middle of the lot and they sat down to keep an eye on the small line of blaze.

"Well, the holidays will soon be here," Chester observed.

Kep didn't say anything. He knew Chester was thinking about his starting to school. The thought of going back to face all the students who knew about him sent a feeling of sickness all through him. However, sooner or later the matter was going to have to be settled, he knew that, and had thought about it a lot. It couldn't be put off indefinitely. Certainly the principal would not recommend that he stay out of classes any longer.

Chester cleared his throat. "You'll have to go to school after the holidays, Kep." His tone was nervously dry and apologetic, but it was plain that he was in dead earnest about it. "I've been thinking about your drawing. You're good at that—really good. The talent you have for it should be developed. So with that in mind, I've decided that the best thing would be for you to start in school over at the town of Beverly. It's only about fourteen miles from here. They've got a good high school, and I've learned that you can take art there." He stood up and smiled. "That suit you?"

"Yes, sir," Kep said gratefully. "I sure appreciate that."

144

"Good. Transportation will be no problem for there's a paved road. We'll work that all out later." He walked away to where the small line of the grass fire was slowly eating its way across the lot and fiddled at helping the fire do its job.

Watching him, Kep felt a great surge of affection for the man. At last, it seemed, they were beginning to understand each other better. So great was his gratitude for the consideration Chester had shown him in the matter of school that his eyes suddenly blurred.

As CHESTER had said, when the holidays were past, he took Kep to the town of Beverly and registered him in school. From the first Kep was happy there. He liked everything about the school, especially his art classes. During that very first day he decided his future. Someday he was going to be a commercial artist; he would never let anything change his mind on that.

Chester met him after school, and all the way home Kep told him enthusiastically about his first day at the new school. Chester was immensely pleased that the problem of Kep's schooling had now been solved.

Another of his fears gone, Kep again felt much the same as he had when Link had freed him from his fear of guns. He took one look at Oda when they walked

145

into the house, saw her as always locked in her emotional shell, and as always his heart ached for her. He determined to try harder than ever to help her.

Saturday morning after breakfast he went to his room for some drawing practice. About ten o'clock he put his drawings aside and picked up an outdoor magazine he had bought at Beverly but hadn't read yet. Then he went out and settled himself by the fireplace in the living room. In a few minutes Oda came in and started her dusting.

As he read, Kep watched her going about her housework in methodical silence, and a feeling of fullness and warmth grew in him for this woman he wanted so much to think of as his mother. He stood up and took a step toward her.

"I was just thinking about something," he said, slapping his leg with the rolled-up magazine. "There's a movie they've got on in town. It's a kind of a musical picture like, a lot of singing and dancing...a lot of life to it, I reckon. I like a picture that's got a lot going on, don't you? We could go to see it. Be a good way to spend the afternoon, because it's too cold to do anything but stay inside anyway."

She turned from the mantle and started across the room. Then as though his voice had just caught up with her, she stopped and turned to him. After a long moment her eyes took on light and her mind came back from wherever it stayed most of the time.

"What did you say?" she asked him.

They stood stone-still facing each other, their senses aware in the warm atmosphere of the room, the boy who had known a devastating grief and the woman who had known the same kind of grief but whose mind and spirit no longer had the resiliency of youth that is able to withstand such emotional stress.

When she said nothing, Kep ran his tongue over his lips in embarrassment. "I just thought maybe—well—that it would be a good idea if we went to see that movie with the singing and dancing in it. I heard it was a right good show."

A faint, very faint smile flickered across her thin lips. Then it was gone. "Thank you, Kep. It was nice of you to ask me. But I don't think I'll go." Her hands were making jerky movements with her dust cloth and she looked down at them until they quieted. "You go ahead, if you want to." Her voice was soft and gentle when she said that, then the brittleness returned suddenly as she lifted her head and said sharply, "Go on! Get your things on and go!" She crossed the room and began dusting hurriedly.

Kep went to his room and got his cap and jacket. When he returned to the living room she was not there.

147

He went outside and headed for town, his head bent against the bitter cold wind, his chin drawn down into his jacket collar.

SLOWLY AND RELUCTANTLY winter gave way to timid spring. The south winds hopefully touched the tender young buds in the thickets, and dainty ground flowers carpeted the timbered slopes where dogwood, laurel and firecherry flamed. Then summer was not long in coming.

AT DAWN a ground wind pushed down the ridges, flowing in waves like an invisible surf. A young mother fox came down on the wind, a shadowlike creature slipping swiftly along. She stopped to test the cool air with her sharp muzzle, then raced on in a zigzag course through scrub growth that fringed the valley.

She raced along through the graying dawn light, came to a clump of sumac and stopped to look across a spread of pasture at the dark farm buildings. There was no light in any of the buildings nor any movement anywhere, except in the apple tree near the barn.

The vixen left the clump of sumac and ran swiftly beneath a low layer of ground fog, moving like the wind, and came within striking distance of the apple tree. The dawn was rising fast now.

A big white rooster was the first of the chickens to

flap down out of the apple tree. Then others followed, two and three at a time. All the roosters stopped to crow before starting the day's foraging. Then the big white one approached the place where the vixen was hiding, running on his toes and working his wings.

The vixen shot out of the weeds, a red blur of motion, killed the rooster neatly with one bite, picked it up and whirled away toward the marsh thicket. Even as she spun away she saw the burst of fire in the dark shadows at the corner of the low shed, and a hot stabbing jolt struck her in the side, staggering her.

She raced through the ground mist, flashed along the sheltered fence row and flew up the slope into the timber. It was there that the first loss of strength caught up with her. She stumbled, swayed and came to a stop beside a tall pine. She swept her gaze over her back trail. A dog was loping around the marsh, bellowing with each jump, and a man was moving about the barnyard. The dog was a farm dog, not a hound. The vixen wasn't worried about it.

She lapped at the wet, sticky patch on her side for a moment then picked up her rooster and trotted on up the slope, the agony in her side dragging at her. She came to a patch of buckbrush, fell into it and lay panting. After a long time, when she thought she had regained some strength, she got to her feet, picked up her burden and went on at a walk.

KEP WAS WALKING along the high hump of the ridge, breathing in the warm air. A bluejay, so nearly the color of the sky that it was hardly noticeable, streaked across his line of vision, calling raucously. A fresh breeze husked along the flat top of the ridge.

When he saw the fox down the slope, Kep froze against the boulder. He watched the vixen grading up the ridge, swaying, pausing, then going on. As he watched, her front legs suddenly gave way and she dropped the rooster. Then she slid her chin in the leaves and stayed there, legs splayed. Kep knew by the dark patch of blood on her side that she had been shot. He knew too that she was trying to make her den with her kill because she had cubs there.

Finally she got to her feet, sniffed at the rooster and went on without it, half walking, half dragging herself. Kep watched her struggle toward the top of the ridge, falling again and again. Finally she fell and rolled over on her side. Kep knew instinctively that she wasn't going to get up again. He moved slowly and silently toward her. When he was ten feet from her he saw the den, an old woodchuck hole that was completely surrounded by brush except for a small dust wallow at the mouth of it. There on the bare patch of ground, bracing itself, little black forelegs spread and tiny muzzle lifted, was a single cub.

150

As Kep watched, the little animal started toward where the dead vixen lay. The cub hadn't seen her yet but had scented her and the strange smell of her blood. Then it stopped suddenly as something in its imagination frightened it. It spun around and went tumbling toward the den, yipping and whimpering.

The cub stopped on the dust patch and looked back. It haunched, yipped a few times, then started toward its mother again. It moved cautiously, feeling its way with its muzzle, keen young senses reading the wind. Finally it saw the dead vixen, began to run, fell in its eagerness and rolled like a ball of yarn. It got up, looked around to get its bearings, then ran on to her. The cub came in boldly, whining and growling, and began to nurse.

If the vixen had been alive Kep would have laughed aloud at the cub's eagerness and the bullying baby way it went about getting its dinner. Knowing the mother was dead, it was a hurting thing to see, a touching of a sore place deep inside himself that could not stand to be touched.

He started walking slowly toward the cub. Its eyes were half-closed in the ecstasy of nursing and it didn't see him until he was almost upon it. Then it stopped nursing and stared at him curiously for a moment before it let out a growl, ran to the den, scooted across the dusty patch and disappeared. Kep squatted down and

151

touched the vixen. The warmth was now leaving her body. She was young; this single cub was no doubt her first litter. He picked the body up and laid it on a stump. Then he put the rooster on the stump too and started down the ridge at a trot, heading for Link's house. When he got there, he ran across the back yard and up on the back gallery.

"Hi, there!" Link called from inside the house. "Come on in." He was in his bedroom, and called out, "Well, your school term is over, how did you do? You haven't been over to tell me."

"Oh, all right, I reckon," Kep told him. "My report card wasn't too bad."

"I bet it was darn good. What did your folks think of it?"

"Well, Chester thought I did real good for going only a half term."

"And Oda?"

"I don't know what she thought. I left my report card on the table where she could see it. I was hoping she'd look at it, but I don't know if she did or not. Anyhow, she didn't say anything about it."

Link came out of his bedroom then, in a clean shirt and trousers, carrying a suitcase.

"Hey, what's going on?" Kep asked him.

"I'm going to drive around over the state for a few

days and see if I can pick up some merchandise. I've got to have some stock for the summer."

"How long will you be gone?"

"A week. Maybe two."

"I got a surprise for you! Kep said excitedly. "I know where there's a baby fox." He told Link about the vixen and her cub, then said, "I'm going to take a shovel and go back and bury the vixen."

"Her hide's no good?"

"No, she's been shot all full of holes. You know what? I want to make a pet of that cub. Can it be done?"

"Sure," Link said thoughtfully, "it can be done. But are you real sure you want to make a pet of the little varmint?"

"Oh gosh, yes! I could make a pet of him and he could live right on in the woods. It wouldn't be like keeping a dog. Oda couldn't object if he never came around the house. She'd not even know about him. Why wouldn't it be all right?"

Link was bent over fastening the straps on his old suitcase and now he straightened up and said, "We just have to make the road as hard for ourselves as we can, don't we?"

"I don't get what you mean."

"Boy, if you make a pet of that cub you're letting yourself in for a lot of grief." He shrugged. "But if it was

153

a dog or any other living thing it would be the same, I guess. That's the nature of humans. We let ourselves love something, and it brings us grief." He picked up his suitcase and Kep followed him out to his pickup truck. "You'd better not go making too much of that wild creature," he warned. "He's a fox, and he was born to be wild."

"He can be tamed, can't he?"

"Partly. Maybe half of him can, but the other half will always be wild. He'll be your pal now while he's young, but there'll come a day when you won't mean a thing to him."

"I couldn't just let the little thing stay up there and starve, could I?"

Link looked at him. Seeing how desperately the boy needed a pet, he shook his head and said, "No, I guess you couldn't. I don't see how you could do that. You'd best train him to stay in the woods, though. At first he'll want to follow you wherever you go, but you train him to stay in the hills, because if you don't somebody'll shoot him, or else some dog will work him over."

"I'll do that," Kep said. "I'll train him never to come out of the hills. Wonder what I should feed him." He was following Link back to the house.

"Well, he ought to be ready for meat, though I'd give him some milk too for a while."

"I'll do that. I'll take some stuff up to him right now."

"There's some canned milk in the refrigerator. Better make it about half water. You know where the key for the back door is, so you can fix your stuff here and take it to him. Then you won't have to explain to Oda what you're up to."

"Yeah, that'd be better, all right. You think it's okay to give him some meat?"

"Yes, sure. Get him started on it."

After Link left, Kep mixed some canned milk with water and poured it into a Coke bottle. With that and a bowl and a shovel he hurried back to the hills.

He approached the fox den quietly, but didn't see anything of the cub. He poured the milk in the bowl and placed it near the mouth of the den. Then he took the dead vixen down the slope and buried her. When he went back to the den, the cub hadn't come out yet. So he sat on a log and watched for an hour and still it didn't show itself.

Then Kep got the rooster from the stump where he had put it, cut it up with his pocketknife and placed two small chunks of meat on a piece of bark at the mouth of the den. Next he whistled to the cub. He might as well start training it to know his whistle.

Again he sat on the log and watched the den opening. It wasn't more than five minutes until the odor of the fresh meat brought the cub out. It sniffed around until it located the meat, snatched a piece of it, growling to itself, and ran back into the den. In a few minutes it was back for the other piece. It came out the third time, and when it found no more meat, it smelled the milk in the bowl, gave it a few experimental laps, then drank half of it before waddling back into the den, its sides puffed out.

Kep buried the remains of the rooster and took the Coke bottle and the shovel back to Link's house. That evening he took the cub more milk and some fresh hamburger. Kep stayed out of sight and watched it come out and eat. After it had finished eating and gone back to its den, he went on home.

He went out to feed it twice a day for the next week, and at the end of that time he had the cub coming out for its food while he stood on the bare spot before the den and watched it. Before Link returned, the cub was eating out of Kep's hand.

When Link drove up to his house just before dark one evening, Kep was there, and he helped unload the half dozen pieces of ancient furniture Link had brought.

"Gosh, you didn't get much in two weeks' time," Kep observed.

"I sure didn't," Link agreed. "And none of it too good at that."

"Say, wait till you see my pet," Kep said happily. "He's

getting to be really something! Eats out of my hand."

"Yeah? What do you call him?"

"I named him Topper, because he's getting long legs and he's going to be a fast one, a real ridge topper."

"Well, we'll go up and see him tomorrow," Link said.

"Yeah, I want you to see him," Kep said eagerly. "I'll come over in the morning, and we'll go."

The next morning he brought canned milk and hamburger for the fox and Link watched him prepare the food.

"You're going broke feeding that thing, I'll bet," he said.

"He's sure eating a lot now, all right," Kep admitted. "But it won't be long I reckon until he'll be getting mice and stuff for himself."

"Probably is already. You're just spoiling him."

As they left the house and started up the slope toward the hills, Link said, "Where's the den?"

"Two ridges to the south," Kep told him.

Kep led the way, and when they had climbed the second ridge, he stopped. "Not much farther now."

"Well, you go on ahead of me," Link told him. "If that little scaper gets a whiff of me he'll likely not come out of his hole."

"Okay, but don't get too far behind me," Kep said. "I want you to see how I can call him out."

They walked a hundred yards down the ridge before Kep motioned Link to stop. He went on a few yards farther and also stopped.

He gave a long shrill whistle followed by three short ones. In response, the long-legged fox cub came scrambling out of its den, saw Kep and stood waiting for him. When he came up it started scurrying playfully about him until Kep squatted down and began feeding it. He called back over his shoulder to Link, "Come on up by that stump. I don't think he'll be scared of you. Anyway, I want him to get to know you."

Grinning, Link came on to the stump and Kep walked over there. Together they watched the cub eat.

"He's a patch fox," Link said.

"What's that?"

"That spread of dark fur across his shoulders. He's going to be a beautiful animal. They call them patch foxes. You very seldom see one."

"He's a swell pet, all right!" Kep said. "I believe I like him even better than I would a dog."

"Yeah, there's something different about having a wild thing for a pet. I tamed rabbits and squirrels and just about everything when I was a kid. There's something kind of secret and exciting about making a pet of a wild thing that you don't experience with a domestic animal. You sort of get so you can sense the spirit of the hills in them."

158

"You sure can," Kep agreed. "Let's go up closer now. I saved some of the hamburger for you to feed to him."

As they moved a few steps nearer the den, the cub stopped eating and turned its straw-gold eyes on them for a moment before it went back to its food. They stood where they were a few moments then moved in closer, then stopped, then moved closer still. Before they left, Link had the cub eating out of his hand.

As they started for home Link stopped and looked back. "Yes, he'll get so he loves you with a secret wild kind of love that no domestic animal would ever give you. Then someday he'll forget that you ever existed."

"Will he, sure enough?"

"You bet he will. It would take a good many generations to get all of the wildness out of a fox."

The sun was setting as they came to the top of the second ridge, and they could smell the twilight moving up out of the bottoms. Link paused to look at a tumbled mountain of clouds crouched in the distant sunset glow.

"It's a good thing to stand and look out across space, you know that?"

"Makes you feel kind of puny, don't it?" Kep said. "About like an insect or something."

"Yes, human beings seem pretty small against depth and width, all right. But man is quite a remarkable little insect, when you think of what he has accomplished, against what he had to start with."

They stood in silence gazing at the western horizon where the light was fading behind the pine-wooly backs of the lower slopes. A farm dog barked somewhere. A cowbell tongued twice and was silent.

"While we're standing here philosophizing," Link grinned, "this insect's got an empty feeling in the pit of his stomach."

"This one too," Kep agreed.

They went on, walking side by side, down into the cooling twilight.

chapter fifteen

TOPPER IN TROUBLE

All through the summer, when there was no garden or lawn work or anything else to be done around the Maskew home, Kep would spend his time with Link.

They made many fishing trips to the lake and to Badger Creek. Once they walked six miles over the hills to Rocky Branch, where they found the fishing excellent.

Almost every time they went into the hills Topper would show up, coming up behind them or leaping suddenly from a clump of brush ahead of them. He would trot along beside them like a dog, nuzzling Kep for food. Sometimes when they would lounge on a grassy spot in the shade the fox would come and lie down with them, waiting to be coaxed into a scuffle.

When Link was away in his truck in search of antiques, Kep would go into the hills alone. He and Topper would lie on the grass beneath a tree and look out across the silent distances of the valley, each in his own world, but the two worlds fused into one by the sunny silence of the hills.

At such times Kep would wonder about his future with the Maskews. Would he ever become a real member of the household? He doubted that he would. He loved both Chester and Oda. Chester for how good he had been to him and Oda because he understood how much she suffered from the sadness and the lost feeling that was always with her. He understood exactly how she felt for he had felt that way until he got to know Link.

After thinking about the Maskews, trying to find answers where there were no answers, he would turn his thoughts to his surroundings. He would wish for a piece of paper and a pencil so he could draw a picture of Topper, or a bluejay on a lone pine, or the shady slope of a timbered ridge.

In the late afternoon he would tell Topper good-bye, unless the fox had already wandered away, and he would hurry home to help Chester with any chores that he might want done. He would run down the slope, breathing in the cool, earthy dampness that had gathered in the low places.

Summer rode hot and clear over the land, the sun-washed wind plucking dust from the dusty country roads, the heat pulling growing things up to their full height, the sun leaving its evening colors on the fruit in the orchards, and the lazy creeks and rivers sleeping the days away.

Then another autumn came easing down the hills, spreading its gaudy colors across the woodlands, drying the cotton stalks and sending countless wagonloads of the white fluff to the gins. It shrouded the timbered slopes in good-smelling brushfire smoke, sent boys and girls back to schoolrooms and turned the air brittle with the promise of early frost.

On a Saturday morning, a month after the opening of school, Kep went into town and headed for the meat shop to get some hamburger and meat scraps for Topper. He was thinking that he might stop at Link's and get his rifle. Link had gone off in search of antique furniture again, though he was due back any day. Anyway Kep always knew where the back door key was hidden in the lean-to shed by the workshop.

As he passed the barber shop there were several men talking inside. Glancing in, Kep recognized Otie Hatburn and two other men he and Link had sat around hill fires with on several fox chase nights.

"We'll get him," Otie was saying in his loud voice.

163

"I'm gettin' me some ca'ridges for my squirrel gun to-day."

Another man said, "Ever'body as has got a hound ought to git out and help."

"How'll you know when you got the right one?" someone asked.

"Why, you can tell that devil easy," Otie told him. "He's a patch. The only one I've ever seen around here. You couldn't mistake him."

That was all Kep heard of the conversation as he sauntered on down the street. He entered the drugstore and ordered a strawberry soda with marshmallow. He wondered idly what the men in the barber shop had been talking about. Hunting, he supposed, but what had Otie Hatburn meant by, "He's a patch"?

Suddenly Kep knew what he had meant! A chill of fright ran over him that made the skin of his face and the back of his neck feel as stiff as if it were coated with dried plaster. He slid off the stool, paid for the soda that he hadn't finished, and walked quickly back to the barber shop. Otie Hatburn was gone and so were the other men who had been there.

Kep hurried down the street looking for Otie but couldn't find him. He had to find him! He had to know if Otie had been talking about a patch fox. The first time Link had seen Topper he had said he was a patch fox. Now Otie had said—

Panic, bitter and hot, was sawing around inside of him as he hurried along the street, not really knowing why he was hurrying. If only Link were home. Then he wondered if maybe he was home by now. He ran down Hanover Street to the end of the pavement. From there he could see that Link's pickup was not in front of his gate. He turned and walked back to the town square, and as he passed the hardware store he found someone who could answer him.

One night last winter when he and Link had gone to the hills to listen to the hounds, he had got acquainted with a boy about his own age named Roscoe. He was the son of one of the hound-dog men there at the fire. Now Roscoe stepped out of the hardware store with a new .22 rifle over his shoulder.

Kep stopped and said, "Hi, Roscoe. Got you a new .22?"

"Sure have," Roscoe said happily. "I'm fixin' to shoot me a fox, too."

"What do you mean?" Kep asked. "You don't shoot foxes. They're for chasing."

"We're goin' to shoot this one. He's a bad one, been killin' everybody's chickens out in the valley."

"How do you know what fox it is?" Kep asked.

"Lot of fellers have seen him. I saw him once; he's a patch fox. First one that's ever been around here, so he's the one, all right. He acts like he's crazy or somethin'.

165

Comes right into folks' yards, almost. Seems like he ain't afraid of humans at all. All the hunters around are goin' out after him tomorrow. I'm sure hopin' I get me a shot at him."

Roscoe hurried away but Kep stood stunned. There was no doubt whatever that Roscoe had been talking about Topper. Now Kep turned and started walking along the street, thinking hard how he could save his pet. He didn't know how he could possibly do it. But somehow he must! It was his own fault that Topper was going to be shot, for he had taught the fox not to be afraid of people. He should never have made a pet of the cub. Link had said he shouldn't. But that was past now. He had looked after the fox when he was a baby and he must look after him now. He simply couldn't just let him be killed.

He hurried to the meat shop and got a pound of hamburger and some meat scraps, then ran to Link's house. In the lean-to by the workshop he found a burlap sack, and with it and a piece of sash cord and his package of meat he headed for the hills.

He came to the ridge where he usually called his fox in and walked a half mile along the top of it whistling for his pet. Now there was no sign of the little animal. He took the wrapper off the meat and dropped it unwrapped into the burlap sack so the wind would carry its scent. He walked another half mile along the ridge, then graded down toward the creek.

At the bottom of the slope he began to run. Time was getting short. The sun would be at noon pretty soon, and it was harder to raise the fox in the middle of the day, and in the afternoon. If he didn't find him before dark Topper would probably be killed, for the men would most likely start their hunt early in the morning.

He clawed his way through brush and slogged across wet patches of bottom ground, giving his whistle as he went. He was filled with despair and the lonely feeling that all about him was nothingness; nothing real at all, nothing solid for his feet to stand on.

He ran along one side of the creek for a mile then crossed it and ran back down the other side. By then exhaustion had so deadened his legs that twice he stumbled and nearly fell. He crossed the creek once more and climbed the ridge to the south, never stopping his whistling. When he reached the top of the ridge he had to stop to rest. Noon came and went, and the afternoon hours crept by. About a half-hour before sunset, weary, hungry and discouraged, about ready to give up, Kep was walking along the ridge toward Morton's Knob when he saw the fox standing beside a leafless bush.

"Well, at last!" he cried, and sat down on the ground. "Come on over here."

The fox came leaping toward him and they had their usual tussle. When the romp was over, the fox haunched and watched Kep take the meat out of the sack. Then, petting the fox while he ate, as he always did, Kep slipped the rope around his neck and knotted it.

When Topper finished eating and became aware of the rope, he backed and shook his head in fright. Kep talked to him, trying to calm him, but the fox tugged with all his might against the rope and kept shaking his head, his eyes now red with fright. After several minutes Kep was able to get his arm around him and slowly work the sack over his hindquarters. He dropped the fox into the sack and securely tied the top. Then he shouldered the sack and started for Link's house. As he walked along he was thinking how the fox had become his friend when he had wanted badly to have a pet. Now it would never like him again, never trust him again. But it couldn't be helped. He just had to save the little animal's life. Now he could. He was sure Link would gladly agree to take him a long way from here and turn him loose in another section of the hill country.

As he approached Link's house he peered through the gathering twilight to see if the pickup was parked at the front gate, but it wasn't. He went in the back way and put his burden down, felt the mouth of the sack to be sure it was still tied securely, then went into the workshop and found the flashlight Link always kept there.

He opened the door of the lean-to and took Topper in, leaving him in the sack while he moved some of the lumber and crates outside. After that he got some burlap sacks for Topper to sleep on, fastened the door of the shed and let the fox out of the sack. As soon as he was out, the little animal began excitedly running around and around the small space, snuffing the ground. Kep tried to calm him but the fox was completely indifferent to him. His only interest was in smelling out this strange place.

For a half-hour Kep sat on the ground trying to talk some of the excitement out of his pet but he couldn't, so he carefully slipped out the door and bolted it. To make it doubly safe, he found a piece of wire and wired the hasp. He stood a moment listening to the whisper of the frightened little feet scurrying about the earth floor of the shed. Then he walked out of the yard and headed for home.

When he got there he found that Oda had left his supper on the kitchen table as she sometimes did when he was late. After he had eaten, he went quietly down the hall to his room. He got into bed wearily and was almost asleep when an electric current of apprehension brought him wide awake. What if Link came home in the night and, not knowing the fox was in the lean-to, opened the

169

door to put some of his purchases in there? He might let Topper out. Kep debated whether or not he should go back and put a note on the door of the lean-to, but before he could decide he was sound asleep.

The sun was high when he awoke the next morning. He could hear no one moving about in the house. Chester would probably be gone to church by now and Oda would be doing her housework. He made his own breakfast, wrapped some food scraps in a newspaper, got his jacket from his room and left.

He came into Link's yard the back way and ran to the corner of the house where he could see the front gate. The pickup was not there. He took a deep breath of relief. Link wasn't home, so Topper hadn't been let out.

He hurried to the lean-to and called, "Hi, feller!" as he walked up. "How you doing this morning?"

The wire was still in place around the hasp but as he started to untwist it, some instinct that he couldn't explain made his hands shake. He jerked the wire out of the hasp and opened the door.

There was a hole where the fox had tunneled out beneath the boards of the outer wall. There were some red hairs and some claw marks at the bottom of the boards but Topper was gone!

chapter sixteen

FOX HUNT

Kep hurriedly gathered up his rope and bur-
lap sack, wrapped his food scraps in the sack and tied it
with the rope. Tucking this bundle and his jacket under
his arm, he started for the hills at a run. He ran up the
draw back of Morton's Knob and headed for the next
ridge. He would take them as they came, the hollows
and the ridges, and he would cover them all.

Sadness and frustration made a sick hollowness in his
stomach that pushed bitterly up into his throat so that
he had to keep swallowing against it. Kep didn't know
what time the hunters would start out but he knew he
must hurry because the hunt was sure to be in the day-
time, since they were going to shoot the fox. Of course,
they could get him at night, if he holed up and they

could smoke him out. And Topper would be tired e-
nough that he would be sure to hole up if the chase went
into the night.

Kep came to a place on the skirt of a ridge where he
had often fed the fox. Today he hung the burlap sack
with the food in it in a bush and concealed himself in
the brush as he had done many times before. It was a
kind of game they played. He would hang the food in a
bush while he hid and watched for the fox to find it.
Then he would rush out and scuffle with him before
feeding him. This time the boy waited for more than an
hour and Topper didn't show up. So he stood for fifteen
minutes whistling, but nothing happened.

Kep's heart was banging with sick hurry as he went
up the hollow, tearing his way through buck brush and
thick reed growth. He crossed a valley cotton patch
where he could see a long way down between the rows
but he saw nothing of his fox. He headed up another
ridge, clawing his way through wild berry vines and
ground brush.

The air was chilly enough that he kept his jacket buttoned up as he tramped the hills and hollows. He kept
at it till noon, stopping every few minutes to give his
whistle, knowing every time he did it that there was little chance he'd ever be able to lure the fox close enough
to capture him again, after scaring him as he had yester-

day. He might never get a look at the animal again. A fox wouldn't forget an experience like that. Maybe after a while he'd tame down but not right away.

But he had to find him, Kep kept telling himself, even if it was after he had holed up. Even then he might be able to talk the men out of killing him, if he told them the fox was his pet, and promised them to take him a long way off. If only Link were home, he would be able to handle the situation.

Kep didn't think he had ever been so hungry in his life before, but there was nothing he could do about it. He ran on and on, giving his whistle, stopping every little while to listen, praying in his heart that his little pet wouldn't have to die. His deep hurting became stronger and stronger.

It was past noon when he stopped and sat down beneath a pine tree to rest. Sitting there he heard a sound that caused him to spring to his feet and cup a hand behind his ear. He wasn't sure at first, but then he was. It came clearly up from the south against the chilly breeze. It was the familiar babbling wail of a hound pack. They were far to the south but working northward. The sound that had meant excitement and pleasure so many times was now an alien and hateful thing that brought a feeling of bitterness and intense anxiety.

He stood tensely listening to the mournful *owak!*

173

owak! coming closer. Then the pack veered westward and he could tell that they weren't yet close to the fox because there wasn't enough eagerness in their voices.

Well, all he could do was try to keep within hearing distance of them so that when the fox holed up maybe he could get there in time to save him. He was sure the fox the pack was chasing was Topper. Since the men were intending to kill the patch fox, they would make sure they were onto the right fox before unleashing their dogs.

Kep headed west along the top of a ridge, going at a jog-trot through the timber, but the hound babble was soon out of hearing. He sat down to wait and listen. In about an hour he heard them coming up from the south again. This time when they veered it was to the east, and they were so close he could distinguish each dog's voice. He was on his feet, eyes searching the slant of the ridge for the swift dark streak that would be far out ahead of the pack. When the dogs continued eastward he knew he wouldn't get a glimpse of the fox, for already they were over beyond Black Hollow.

In his troubled mind Kep was saying, *Run, Topper! Run, boy! Don't hole up. If you do they'll kill you! Please don't hole up!*

Three times during the next four hours the sweet

174

chop-mouth trail song came within Kep's hearing, then swerved away, and each time a little more weariness crept into the chorus. Then just as the sun was sinking they came in from the west again, sounding this time as if they were coming up the hollow south of the ridge where he stood.

Suddenly something happened to the baying. Instead of the long contented tones, the pack abruptly started giving out with sharp yips of frustration and disappointment. Something had happened to the trail. Hope pounded through Kep with every thud of his pulse, the hope that they had lost the scent for good.

He ran down the slant of the ridge and concealed himself in a thicket. In less than ten seconds he saw a swift movement that came to a stop a hundred feet from where he was crouched. It was a fox, but it wasn't Topper! It was a slim, graceful young vixen.

Kep remembered then that Link had once told him how one fox will cross trail for another. Now he was sure what had confused the pack; this young vixen had crossed trail for Topper. His heart ached with love for the little animal and what she had done.

The dogs were still down there trying worriedly to straighten out the trail and here, unconcernedly sitting on her haunches, her pointed muzzle delicately tasting the breeze, was the cause of their bumbling. As Kep watched, she daintily lifted first one forepaw then the other and cleaned them with her tongue.

Suddenly a note of confidence came into the pack chorus and a moment later they were again on trail. The vixen seemed to know that it was her trail they had settled on, and confidently, daintily, seeming hardly to touch the ground, she sped away, vanishing instantly into the brush.

Kep watched the hounds stream up the slope, following her trail, lining out as they passed him, pounding away through the undergrowth. There was hope in his heart now as he listened to the fading trail song. If only the vixen could keep them in tow until Topper was rested, he'd have a good chance of losing the pack.

The wind became cooler and Kep turned his jacket collar up as he stood a moment listening to the pack working eastward. Then he started down the slope to the brush-cluttered hollow, then followed the creek.

A few minutes later he heard the pack swing southward. Then he heard something else. A gunshot! He stopped dead, listening. He had known the hunters would station themselves throughout the hills wherever they thought they might get a shot at the fox, but this was the first time a gun had spoken. Were the dogs still after the vixen or had Topper now crossed for her? He stood with pounding pulse listening to the baying, fearing to hear them break the refrain into babbling eagerness, for that would tell him the fox was dead or wounded. When there was no change in their mournful refrain he drew a long breath of relief and walked on.

The pack didn't go very far south this time and there was still some twilight left when they headed north again. Kep climbed a few yards up the slope and sat down with his back against a stump, facing away from the cold wind. Then again the hound chorus broke, shattering abruptly into clumps of high-pitched single notes of disappointment.

Kep was thinking that Topper had probably crossed trail for the vixen this time, and at that moment a breath of swift motion caught his attention. It was a mere shadow flashing through the twilight down near the creek. It was gone for a moment, then it showed again. When it stopped near a clump of brush, even in the half-light Kep could tell that it was Topper!

The little animal's coat was shaggy from thorn tears, and his brush was matted with burrs. His tongue was hanging out and his chest was pumping like a bellows. Kep wanted to cry, seeing how weary and miserable his pet looked.

Topper stood for a moment, muzzle lifted, then trotted along the creek bank a few yards and stopped beside

177

a thick-trunked oak that sat on the very edge of the bank just above the water line. He sniffed the trunk of the tree then trotted on along to a place where the shore slanted down to the water. There he hesitated a moment before he doubled back toward the oak tree, walking at the very edge of the water, and disappeared behind the cutbank.

Kep thought the fox was going to swim the creek in an effort to throw the hounds off his scent, but he didn't. He just disappeared. Kep started to call to him, but some instinct told him not to. He kept watching and the fox did not swim the creek. Then Kep knew what had happened. Topper had waded at the edge of the water to kill his scent and had holed up beneath the big oak, where there must be a den that he had known about.

Kep walked down to the creek and lay on his stomach at the edge of the cutbank where he could see the den entrance beneath the oak. He smiled at the cleverness of his fox. Under there, Topper would have a good chance of fighting off a whole pack of hounds because the only way the dogs could approach the den would be from the water, which was too deep for them to wade; they'd have to do their fighting while swimming.

What the fox didn't know was that after the hounds told the men where the quarry was the men could wade to the other side, shine a light into the den and put a bullet between the two gleaming eyes that the beam would reveal.

Kep realized this and panic seized him. He must do something! The moment the hounds got the trail straightened out they would come pounding down the creek bank, the men not far behind them. It probably wouldn't take the pack long to find the trail again. Somehow he must completely kill Topper's scent so the dogs couldn't possibly find him. But how? His mind became a whirling pinwheel of anxiety as he tried to think what he should do.

He rose to his feet and walked back along the edge of the bank. Suddenly the bank caved off and he was in water way above his knees. As he scrambled out an idea came to him and he knew how he could save Topper.

If only he had the burlap sack he had hung in the brush a mile down the ridge, but there was no time to get it. Frantically his eyes searched the creek bank for some bunch grass, but there was none. As a thought came to him, he quickly took everything out of the pockets of his pants and jacket and put the stuff on a stump before he yanked his jacket off.

Kep ran to the spot where Topper had walked along the edge of the creek, and stepped down into the water, which chilled him as it climbed up his legs. There was an eight-inch ledge along the bottom of the cutbank that

the fox had used to get to the den. Kep soused his jacket
in the water and, using it like a mop, waded along swab-
bing the ledge to obliterate the fox's tracks. When he
came to the tree roots the water was up to his armpits.
He could see the mouth of the den but it was too dark to
be able to see the fox.

"Stay right there, boy," he whispered into the den.

He went back to mopping the ledge again. When he
finally climbed out of the water and the wind struck him
he began to shiver.

Now he worked along the upper bank, slapping the
ground with the wet jacket, trying to blot out completely all scent of the fox. He worked in a frenzy of haste,
running to wet the jacket, then running back to swab
the ground, praying in his heart as he worked, praying
earnestly for his pet to be saved.

Once he stumbled at the edge of the creek and
plunged face-down into the water. He struggled up,
gasping and coughing. Hurry! Hurry! Hurry! His teeth
chattered, his breath clawed its way in and out of his
throat as he was slapping the ground, scrubbing it,
wanting to cry at each thought of losing his pet, the one
thing he could call his own.

Maybe the water he had been able to splash over the
ground with his jacket wouldn't be sufficient to keep
the sharp-nosed hounds from picking up the scent. He
stopped and listened to the distant baying of the hounds.

They were still bumbling around trying to pick up a clear trail. Chilled to the bone now, he decided to build a fire and dry himself out. That was when the real solution came to him. He believed he knew for sure now how he could save his fox!

He ran to the stump where he had put the stuff from his pockets and got a pad of matches. Then frantically he began gathering dry leaves and twigs, crawling a-round on his hands and knees, groping for anything dry enough to burn. When he had both hands filled, he went upwind from the den tree, made a mound of leaves and twigs and struck a match. A tiny flame leaped to life and by its light he quickly gathered more fuel.

Something was nagging at his consciousness and he had to stop what he was doing before he could think what it was. The hounds! They had the trail again now and were coming down the creek! Hearing them he be-came a wild person, running about within the glow of his fire snatching at anything he could see that would burn. If only he could get the fire built up enough—! Stumbling, stooping, snatching, sobbing, hoping, pray-ing that the hounds would lose the trail again.

They didn't lose it. He could hear them clearly now. Soon they would come plunging out of the darkness a-long the creek bank. He threw an armload of brush onto his fire and it blazed high, but that wasn't the kind of fire he wanted. So he ran to a big tree that was hollow to the ground and dug wildly in it until he came up with both hands full of damp leaves which he threw on the fire. Instantly the blaze went down and the breeze caught its cloud of smoke. He stood a moment to see if it was aimed right. It was. The smoke was hovering close to the ground and spreading along the bank— straight toward the tree where his fox was holed up, and on down the bank in the direction Topper had come.

He ran to the hollow tree for more wet leaves. He made still a third trip, and now his fire was a smudge, just the way he wanted it. It was laying a thick cloud of acrid smoke all along the creek bank. The hounds would never be able to pick a scent out of that fog.

A few yards up the creek he found a spongy old log from which he broke several chunks and ran with them to the fire. They were just what he needed to keep the smudge alive. He hoped he wasn't making the smoke so strong that it would compel Topper to leave his den.

The woods were full of hound babble now, and suddenly the pack arrived, running hard, bunched up, hurtling out of the smoke fog, skating on their noses, slobbering and sneezing, flinging themselves about in senseless confusion. They aimed their muzzles at the sky to moan their ill luck, they circled, they tried to get something into their nostrils besides the smoke of the fire.

Behind the pack came two men carrying lanterns and

guns. They came up to Kep's fire through the smoke, coughing and hawking. Kep recognized them. They were Tom Kepley and Cleve Wilford, men he had seen a couple of times around a hilltop fire.

"Say, what is this?" Kepley gasped as he pawed his way out of the choking smoke cloud.

Cleve Wilford stopped on the windward side of the fire, jerked his head to shake the smoke tears from his red eyes and said, "What you doin', boy?"

"Trying to get dried out," Kep grinned. "Creek bank caved off with me. Built me a fire to get dry by."

"That ain't no fire," Kepley snorted. "You won't never git dry with no more blaze than that."

"Who are you? What're you doin' out here?" Wilford asked.

"I'm Kep Lanning. I live in town. I've seen you men around a ridge fire a time or two."

"Yeah, I recollect you now," Kepley said. "You was with Link Wybel."

"That's right."

"What yuh doin' out here?" Wilford asked again.

"Listening to the chase. A lot of times I wander into the hills when I hear hounds. Like to listen to them."

The dogs were all quiet now, lolling around the puny fire, lapping at their briar and brush wounds, satisfied to let this be the end of the chase.

183

"Wonder what happened to that fox trail?" Wilford asked dolefully as he tamped tobacco into an old black pipe.

"If that fox ran through this smoke, the dogs won't never find him tonight," Kepley said disgustedly. "Anyhow, the dogs have all got a snootful of it. Won't none of them be able to smell nothin' for an hour or two. We might's well hit out for home."

Wilford looked the dogs over, some of which were already asleep. "Yeah," he agreed. "You'd never git 'em out onto a trail now."

Without saying any more to Kep, they walked off into the darkness the way they had come, whistling to the pack.

Kep was grinning as he watched them go. In a few minutes he stood up, scraped all the dry leaves and twigs away from his fire and left it smoldering. He started for home, his wet pants slapping about his ankles at every step.

Down the draws and up over the slopes he went, running to try to keep warm. At last he came to Morton's Knob. He took the slope at a dead run, his teeth chattering. There was a light in Link's house and he headed there.

He ran into the yard through the back gate, up onto the back porch, and into the kitchen.

Link was at the stove and the warm room was filled

with the good odors of frying steak and potatoes. He turned from the stove and took note of the soggy clothes, smoke-grimed face and wet, matted hair. "Well, what happened to you?"

"I've had a time!" Kep panted.

"You sure look like you'd had a time. Boy, you're soaked. What did you do, fall in the lake?"

Kep shook his head. "I've been in the creek. I got a lot to tell you."

"You've got to get into dry clothes, that's what you've got to do," Link told him. He put his potlifter down and said, "Come in here."

They went to his bedroom where he gave Kep a shirt and a pair of jeans. "Go get a hot shower and rub down good," he ordered. "I'll have some grub ready in no time. Bring your wet clothes to the kitchen and dry them out by the oven."

By the time Kep returned Link had food on the table. While they ate Kep told Link all that had happened from the time he had heard the men talking in the barber shop. When he finished he said, "Wasn't that a smart trick, finding a den where the dogs couldn't get to him without swimming?"

"Pretty foxy trick you pulled yourself, building that fire," Link grinned. "But it's a wonder you didn't smoke the fox out too."

"The way the wind was, the smoke stayed pretty well

up on top of the creek bank. Didn't go low enough to bother him, I reckon."

An hour later Kep changed into his dried clothes, said good night and headed for home. The house was quiet when he got there so he let himself in the kitchen door and went quietly to his own room.

He lay in bed thinking that tomorrow he would talk to Link about taking Topper away. He wondered how far a fox would range. They might have to take him a hundred miles or more to make sure he wouldn't come back.

His throat tightened at the thought of losing his pet. Still, if the fox wasn't taken away he would be hunted until he was finally killed.

chapter seventeen

THROUGH THE FOG

Kep awakened slowly the next morning to find
that he was very tired. When he first opened his eyelids
just a slit, the light struck pain into his head so he closed
them again. He lay there for a while and watched the
distorted play of light outside his eyelids, then he tried
opening them again slowly. When he turned his head on
the pillow the room went swinging around him. He tried
to swallow and his throat was so dry he couldn't.

His hands gripping the mattress, he sat up on the
edge of the bed and let the aching dizziness drain out of
him. He tried several times more to swallow and when
his throat finally did come open a fit of coughing seized
him.

He got to his feet and again the room whirled. Now

he stood with his legs spread, waiting for it to stop. When he took a step the floor felt rubbery beneath him. He decided he'd better get dressed and go eat some breakfast. Going without food all day yesterday was probably why he felt so bad.

As he went through the living room Oda was there with the vacuum and she gave him her usual nod and two-word greeting. In the kitchen, he fried two eggs and made toast for himself, and drank a cup of coffee with them. But eating breakfast didn't make him feel any better; he still had that hot, pushed-in feeling.

Kep had planned to go to Link's the first thing and talk to him about taking Topper away, but he believed he'd wait until later in the day. He didn't feel like walking that far right now. Best to get limbered up first, maybe work out some of the stiffness that his muscles had soaked up from getting wet last night.

He went outside into the garden plot and began pulling weeds and stacking them. As he worked, the strange, half-sleepy feeling grew in him and the dizziness came again. Every few minutes he would have to stop and cough. He hadn't worked more than an hour when he decided to let the weed pulling go until later when he was feeling better. He sat down on the back porch steps. Soon the sun was too warm there, and that was strange, because the air was cool, the wind brisk out of the northwest.

188

He went to his room to get his drawing pad and pencil and sat on the living room couch to sketch for a while, but he didn't like what he drew. When he stood up he was so dizzy that he had to hold on to the back of the couch for a moment until the room steadied. He went to his room and lay down on his bed with all of his clothes on.

He lay there with his eyes closed until finally the dizziness smoothed out into waves that were like a sheet blowing on a clothesline. Or was it like ocean waves? Yes, that was it. Like the ocean. The bed was like a boat, swaying, with nothing under it. It was frightening at first, but then he didn't mind the waving any more. He sort of liked it. It was restful. So he just let the bed sway and didn't think any more about it. No use thinking about it. No use thinking about anything.

CHESTER CAME HOME at the regular time that evening and found Oda preparing dinner. He asked where Kep was in the casual, half-timid way in which he always spoke to her, forever hopeful that he might someday be able to draw her into a conversation.

Oda said in her quiet colorless tone, "He's home, for a change."

"Where is he?"

"In his room, I suppose."

He went down the hall to Kep's room and called to him but got no reply. He rapped and still got no answer, so he pushed the door open and saw the boy lying on the bed. From the doorway he could hear the heavy raspy breathing. He glanced once at the flushed face, then hurried to the living room and called Doctor Malon's office in Beverly. Dr. Malon had been their family doctor for many years. The doctor's nurse told him the doctor would be there as soon as possible. Chester thanked her and hung up.

Oda, standing in the dinette archway, said worriedly, "He's sick?"

"Yes," Chester told her, and hurried back to Kep's room.

He went in and stood beside the bed a moment listening to the dry labored breathing. When he touched the hot face he could tell the boy's temperature was dangerously high. Kep never even woke up as Chester undressed him and put on his pajamas.

The doctor arrived in less than an hour and Chester showed him to Kep's room. Oda followed them down the hall and stood in the doorway while the doctor made his examination. Nervous anxiety was tightening her thin face. There was no sympathy, no desire to assist, just that drawn, anxious expression.

The doctor finally put his stethoscope away and

looked up at the two of them. "Pneumonia," he said tensely, reaching for his medicine case.

Chester glanced concernedly at Oda, standing like a gray-clad statue in the doorway, then said to the doctor, "Maybe . . . we should have him taken to the Beverly Hospital?"

The doctor shook his head. "This morning I would have sent him to the hospital, but I don't want him moved now."

After he had given his patient a shot of penicillin, Dr. Malon told Chester he wanted a nurse, and Chester phoned for one. Then the doctor called the hospital at Beverly for an oxygen tent. By seven o'clock Kep was under the oxygen tent and the doctor turned him over to the nurse, telling Chester that he had some calls to make in Beverly and would be back at ten.

"Is he—is he showing any improvement, Doctor?" Oda asked him.

Dr. Malon shook his head. "Not yet, Mrs. Maskew. It's too early yet to expect any improvement."

Oda turned away, worry creasing her face, and went to her room. Chester watched her go, then walked to the living room and sank down on the couch and put his head in his hands.

He was living it again now, going through all that he had gone through when his own son died and he knew that Oda was too. There was a difference this time. Before there had been nobody to blame and this time he himself was to blame. If he had never brought Kep here they wouldn't be facing it again. If the boy died, what would happen to her? How could her frightened sorrowing mind ever go through it a second time? He had brought the boy here because he wanted to help her as well as Kep, and now his plan was only causing her more sorrow and worry than ever.

Dr. Malon came again at ten o'clock. He sat a long time listening to Kep's breathing, looking at the long-jawed boyish face with the clay-tan hair falling across the forehead. Once he opened the plastic oxygen tent and looked in, then closed it again.

Abruptly Kep stirred, lifted one hand, then let it fall. A moment later his dry lips moved and his tongue came out to wet them. Slowly he began to talk, and the words were loud enough that Chester and Oda, standing in the hall doorway, could hear them.

"Oda;" he said. "Oda, do you reckon I ought to maybe clean up the furnace room today? Could I do that for you, Oda?"

Chester watched the little lines tighten about his wife's eyes. A nervous tic tugged at the right corner of her mouth. After a moment she turned away, her face bent, and walked silently down the hall to her room.

192

After a few minutes, the doctor went into the hall and motioned Chester to follow him into the living room.

"Ask your wife to come here, please," Dr. Malon said. "I want to talk to her."

Chester's thin face puckered with anxiety. "Well—I don't know, Doctor, whether she'll come out or not. I'll ask her."

He went down the hall and knocked softly on Oda's door before he pushed it open. "The doctor wants you. He's out in the living room. He wants you to come out there." She was standing by a window and didn't turn or speak. "Come on, Oda. He wants to talk to you— maybe to both of us, I don't know."

She turned her lifeless eyes to him. After a moment she walked listlessly into the living room where they sat together on the couch. The doctor was waiting for them.

"The patient was close to regaining consciousness a while ago," he told them. He turned to Oda. "I wish you would go in and talk to him. Just sit and talk to him as if he were awake."

She sat a long moment staring at the doctor, her black eyes as hard and sharp as slivers of ice, then began to shake her head. Her face was twisted with agony.

"He's going to die!" she said, the words bubbling slowly out of her. "He's going to die, and you want me

193

to sit there and watch him die the way—the way I did with Jimmy. I won't do it! You can't make me do it," she said defiantly. Then pitiously, "Please don't make me do it!"

"We don't know that he's going to die," the doctor said soothingly. "We're going to try to help him live. That's why I want you to go to him. Right now he needs to hear your voice."

"I—I can't!" she whimpered.

The doctor was sitting with his forearms on his knees and his long fingers laced together. "Mrs. Maskew, you shouldn't hold onto your grief as you're doing. Think how long it has been since your son died, and yet you're still clinging to your sorrow. That's not good."

Her defiance tightened in faintly quivering lines about her mouth. She sat straight, eyes closed, and slowly shook her head. Finally her lips moved and in her far-away voice she said, "You don't know. No one who hasn't been through it can know. I know. I know what it's like to have a dead soul and to go on living, to go on living with nothing but emptiness and more emptiness."

"You could change," Dr. Malon told her gently, "but you won't let yourself. You won't let yourself smile or laugh or feel happy. That's because you have the absurd notion that if you did you would be breaking faith with your dead son. That's why you won't let yourself love or even notice this other boy—because you think it would be unfair to your own son."

She got to her feet, stood as straight and unyielding as a slender shaft of steel, turned and left the room.

It was a half-hour later that Kep again began talking in his delirium. The doctor was sitting beside his bed, giving quiet instructions to the nurse. Chester and Oda were again standing in the hall just outside the sick room.

"We've got to do it, Link," Kep said, then moaned softly and tried to moisten his parched lips with his tongue. "We've got to get him a long ways off from here, that's for sure." Then he turned his head on the pillow and was silent.

Again the doctor took Chester and Oda down the hall to the living room.

"Do you think he's any better, Doctor?" Oda asked, her eyes frantically searching the physician's face.

He shook his head. "I had hoped for some encouragement by now, but there is none. I suppose you both heard what he just said."

They nodded.

"Who is this Link he's talking about?"

Chester cleared his throat and said hesitantly, "Link Wybel. He's—well, what I suppose you'd call the town pariah. Most every small town has one. He was born here. His parents had a rather unsavory reputation. His father was a mill hand, and they lived in a part of town that no longer exists, called Shack Town. Link left here when he was in his teens. He came back two or three years ago."

"How does your boy happen to know him?"

"I suppose just about every boy in town knows Link," Chester said. "He spends most of his time in the hills, hunting and fishing, and kids seem to just get to know a man like that."

Oda said flatly, "No respectable people in this town would have the man in their house."

The doctor said, "Suppose you ask him to come here at once, Chester."

Chester threw his wife a quick glance. "Do you think it might help the boy if he came?" he asked the doctor.

Dr. Malon looked steadily to Oda. "When we doctor the body," he said gravely, "we don't fail to consider the mind. The boy's got something on his mind that has to do with this Link Wybel. I want him brought here."

"Chester!" Oda said in a tragically demanding tone.

"I'll get him," Chester told the doctor.

Again Oda said, "Chester!"

For a moment their eyes met and held, then he smiled

his quiet apologetic smile. When he spoke there was a firmness in his tone that caused her thin dark brows to lift.

"I'll bring him," he told the doctor again.

Ten minutes later he stopped his car at Link Wybel's gate. He left his headlights on and by their beam was able to thread his way through the junk in the yard.

Link had been reading. When he saw the car stop at the gate, he stood up, stuffed his shirt into his pants and went to the door.

"Well, hello, Mr. Maskew," he greeted when he opened the door and saw Chester coming up the gallery steps. "Come in."

Chester stepped inside. "Hello, Link. How busy are you?"

Link grinned. "I'm about as busy as I ever permit myself to get, which is to say, not busy at all. Have a seat."

"I was wondering if you'd come over to my house with me, Link. Kep is sick."

"Bad?"

"Pneumonia. He's been talking to you in his delirium, and Dr. Malon thought you should come."

"Sure. Just give me a few minutes to change clothes."

In ten minutes Link was back in the living room, shaved and combed, wearing dark trousers, a fresh white shirt, a tie and jacket. "Let's go," he said briskly.

When they arrived at the Maskew home Oda was nowhere to be seen. Link followed Chester down the hall to the sick room and was introduced to the doctor.

The doctor tipped his head toward the sickbed and said, "Talk to him. Let him know it's you. He may not hear you at first but talk to him anyway. Keep talking."

Link nodded and sat down by the bed. He began to talk in the slow, soothing drawl that was as much a part of him as the almost womanly tenderness that lived in his gray dreamer's eyes.

"Kep," he said, "I've been thinking of that day you told me about the bears down in the Florida Everglades. You remember that? Well, thinking about it, I was reminded to tell you about the bears up in Canada. I don't reckon I ever did tell you about hunting grizzlies up there, did I? Well, they're really a lot of bear, those grizzlies."

As he talked he was studying Kep's drawings on the walls of his little room. He recognized the pool where he and Kep had first met.

"Bet you didn't know about a bear's claws, did you?" Link went on. "Now you take a dog or a cat or any other animal; when he works his claws they all work together. A bear, he's different; he can work his claws one at a time, the same as you can your fingers. Why,

198

he can pull leaves and berries off of bushes just as handy as you can."

The nurse and the doctor were absorbedly watching the feverish face beneath the plastic tent, as was Chester, standing in the doorway.

Now Link noticed that Oda had also come to stand in the doorway. As he looked at her, taking note of the fierce anxiety in her dark eyes, he knew it was because she thought this boy was going to die, just as her own son had done.

"Do you know what the Canadian grizzly likes best to eat?" his voice droned on. "Mice, that's what. Mountain mice that live under rocks. They'll go around lifting up rocks, looking under first one then another. Why, I've seen one of those big scapers lift a rock that would take five or six good men to move."

Again his glance moved to Oda's strained face, and he wondered if perhaps this illness of Kep's would be the thing that would make her accept the boy. Maybe seeing him so close to death would open her heart to him. Or maybe it would seal her off from the world forever.

"I'll tell you something about grizzlies, Kep. You've heard how a grizzly will try to get you in a bear hug and crush the life out of you? Well, that's not so. I don't know who ever started that, but a grizzly just won't do it. No, what a grizzly wants to do is get his teeth into you, if he can. Another thing, if he gets close enough to you, he'll throw his paw at you just like a boxer throwing a punch . . ."

On and on he talked, while the others stared at the patient, watching for some sign of returning consciousness.

"You ought to see what a mother bear does with her cubs when danger comes around. You remember how a partridge will put on a crippled act when her young ones are in danger? Well, a mother bear protects her young too, and here's how she does it. When danger shows up she'll haul off and slap her young ones and send them rolling. One after another she'll swing on them, knocking them half out of their senses. They'll get up and scamper into the brush to get away from her, then she'll stand and fight off the enemy, whatever it is, while her kids stay safe out of sight."

His droning, gentle voice was the only sound in the room as he strove to communicate with the sick boy's mind. Link remembered from his own boyhood that the youthful mind needs communion. Or the youthful soul. Or was it that in his reaching out he was searching for himself, always knowing in his heart that the only part of himself he'd ever really find was his youth, and that only in memory.

KEP BECAME AWARE of a tremendous weight on his chest and wondered what it was. Then he saw what it was. A little brown man with a fox face was standing on his chest with a hammer almost as big as himself and he was hitting Kep between the eyes with it. Every time the hammer landed, a rumble like distant thunder would roll out of Kep's head and go bouncing away into nothingness. Then the little brown man started jumping up and down on his chest—up and down! Up and down! Finally he backed off and began throwing little blue footballs at Kep's head. The balls landed regularly between his eyes as the hammer had done and the rumble would again roll out of his head each time one of them struck.

He opened his eyes and the room came partially into focus. Suddenly somebody spun the bed so he closed his eyes, clenched his hands on something soft and clung tightly to it to keep from falling off. Gradually, by squeezing hard on whatever it was he had in his hands, he was able to brake the bed to a stop.

When it was steady, he slowly opened his eyes again and saw a big bear sitting there in the fog. The fog was clear but kind of grayish, and was hanging down all around him. He could see the bear through the fog. He closed his eyes and opened them again and saw that it wasn't a bear at all. It was a man. He wondered where the bear idea had come from.

He looked at his hands. They were right there in front of him and were gripping the bed covers. He slowly turned his head to look at the man through the clear-gray fog. The man said something, and that was the rumbling he had been hearing. The man said a few more words before he stopped and the sound of his voice went rolling away like thunder.

Kep listened intently to the rumbling and was finally able to make out words, though he couldn't tell exactly what they were. He moved his eyes and could see other faces through the fog. The big voice spoke again.

"How you feeling, boy?"

Now he recognized the voice. The man was Link.

Kep tried to speak but his lips were blocks of wood. He ran his tongue out and felt his lips with it. Funny, they didn't feel like anything that belonged to him at all. He could move them, though, so they must belong to him. He tried to swallow and felt the inside of his throat scraping together like shoe soles scuffing on concrete.

Then a face with a white cap above it appeared. Two hands took hold of the fox and lifted it. Something cool touched the blocks of wood that were his lips and he swallowed. The face and the white cap moved away from him and the hands put the fog down again.

He tried to talk, and a funny frog-croak of a voice said the words he had wanted to say, which were: "Link, I been wanting to talk to you."

"Sure, go ahead, boy," Link's thunder-rumbling voice said.

Then that other crazy voice said what he wanted to say again: "Link, we got to get Topper away. They'll get him if we don't."

"Yeah, I been thinking about that," Link's thunder voice said. "Don't you worry. We're going to take care of that scaper, all right."

The big thunder voice said something more but he was too tired now to listen to it. The fog was getting thicker now, and it was nice and cool and soft all around him. It was a fine place to rest, in the nice cool fog. He wondered why he had never thought about sleeping in a fog before.

At midnight another nurse came to relieve the first one. Chester and the doctor went to the kitchen for coffee. Link said he would stay by Kep's bed, so the nurse brought a cup of coffee to him there. A little later the doctor went to bed in Chester's room and Chester dozed on the couch in the living room.

Link sat by the bed all night. Every half-hour Oda would appear at the door to stare in an agony of fear at the sleeping patient, then soundlessly go back down the hall to her room.

Just as dawn light was slipping into the room she came again to the door, hesitated for a moment, then, like a person in a trance, walked into the room and toward Kep's bed. Link stood up and held his chair for her and she sat down, never once taking her eyes from Kep's face. Link stood watching her, smiling.

The doctor came into the room and glanced at Oda. He stepped over and reached beneath the oxygen tent to take hold of Kep's hand. That was all he did, just felt his hand. Then he smiled and patted Oda's shoulder and walked out, motioning Link to follow him. They went to the living room, where Chester was just awakening.

The doctor said to both of them, "The crisis is past. He'll be all right now. I'll have to be going; the nurse can look after him now. I'll be back this evening."

Chester flashed Link a grateful look as he went to the door with the doctor. When he came back to the living room he was smiling and his eyes were bright with the thankfulness he felt.

"I wish there were some way I could repay you, Link," he said.

Link shook his head.

"I know there isn't," Chester said. Then he paused and walked over to a window and stood looking out. "You know, Link, I used to think that having attained the position I have in this town I had just about everything a man could want. I've found out these past few months that I haven't. You have, Link. You have a wisdom and understanding of people that I'll never have. You have succeeded in bringing two people out of the darkness of their own emotions, a thing I tried to do but failed."

Link shoved his hands deep into his trousers pockets in embarrassment. "Well, now, Chester, I never like to hear a man low-rate himself that way. You see, with Kep—well, as a boy my background was about the same as his. So it was easy for me to understand his feelings and kind of figure out the answers to his problems. But, man, you can do a heap more for that boy than I ever could. You can give him a home, and an education —well, you can make a happy family life for him. And for Oda. And for yourself. Me, now, I'll take the boy fishing on occasion. We'll roam the hills some. Set by a hill fire now and then and listen to the hounds being happy on a fox trail. Such as that."

"I wish you would," Chester said, and put out his hand.

They shook hands and Link started out. Then he turned back and said, "How about you going with us once in a while, Chester?"

"I certainly will," Chester assured him. "Thanks for asking me. I don't suppose it's in me to ever be what you might call an ideal father but I'm going to be a better one than I've been in the past, you can depend on that."

Chester watched Link go down the sloping walk, swinging along easily in his catlike stride, a man possessing solidly rooted loyalties and convictions. Then he returned to Kep's room and stood in the doorway a long time watching Oda. She had lifted the edge of the oxygen tent and was holding one of Kep's hands between her own and stroking it.

She smiled at Chester and then looked back at Kep. Chester leaned against the door frame and closed his eyes for a moment in a silent prayer of thanks. His wife was her old self again. It was the first time since their own boy was taken sick that she had smiled. And it was one of the first times since Jimmy's death that she had looked at him with a rational expression.

He walked softly across the room, put his arm about her shoulders and kissed her cheek.

KEP OPENED his eyes, and realized all through his body he felt cool and rested. His mind was perfectly clear now. To wake up feeling rested and without the awful heat in his body was like waking from a bad dream.

He turned his head and saw Oda and Chester there

beside the bed. He lay for a long time just looking at them, wondering why they were there and why she was holding his hand. Why, they were both smiling. It was astonishing. He was further amazed when Oda lifted his hand and pressed it to her cheek.

For a moment he wondered if maybe he wasn't still asleep and dreaming. Then he knew he wasn't. This was real. They were both there by his bed, both smiling at him with love in their eyes! Oda loved him! They both did! He didn't have to be told that they did, he could see it in their eyes and in their smiles.

A hot lump came into his throat as tears of gladness filled his eyes and made everything look shimmery. Then Oda reached under the tent and wiped the tears away and he could see again. Oda and Chester were both still smiling, but there were tears on their cheeks too.